MW01007776

Haitian Gold

Steven Becker

The White Marlin Press

whitemarlinpress.com

steve@stevenbeckerauthor.com

Stevenbeckerauthor.com

Haitian Gold

CHAPTER ONE

My toes lightly gripped the stay at the foot of the foresail, feeling each swell as the *Panther* ran ahead of the wind. I looked aft toward the island barely visible above the horizon and breathed a sigh of relief. There were no sails.

For a flat island, Grand Cayman seemed to take forever to disappear. When it was finally out of sight, the mood of the crew on deck lightened as well. I felt the stay sway as Shayla nimbly moved from the rope ladder to the wooden cross brace to join me. Her warmth enveloped me as her body leaned into mine. This spot, high in the rigging, was my place to think, plan and sometimes brood. It was an odd feeling not being alone, but with Shayla here, it felt right. We had no need to speak. Just being in each other's company was enough. It had been only a week since I had met her—a week that had seen our fortune lost and then recovered, all of us made even richer by the addition of the ton of silver we carried in our hold.

A quick glance at the *Panther*'s sails confirmed the forty-five-foot schooner was well trimmed, and I felt the strain of the past few days fall away. My confidence grew with each passing swell that we would not be pursued by the governor, especially with his man bound in the hold, ready to give testimony in exchange for his life.

Our course was set a hair north of due east and I hoped to see the first of the two smaller islands any moment. We needed a quick repair to the hull, and both islands were rumored to have good anchorages. I had no intention of careening her again; except for the spot that had taken cannon shot from the governor's frigate, the hull was sound.

The wind was fair from the southeast, which made for good sailing, but we were heading into the rainy season and I hoped the weather would serve us well, providing a cloud burst before too long. We had plenty of food, especially with Blue and Lucy manning the lines trolled from the stern. The two small pigmies howled in delight as they pulled in fish after fish. Fresh water was a different matter, though. The Caymans held little and I knew we were running low.

I looked below at the freed slaves, a welcome addition to our previously skeleton crew, working in a chain to stow the treasure deep into the bilge. It had worked for the British, to disguise their wealth from pirates and French privateers; it would work for us as well. Under the supervision of Mason the last of the stones deep in the keel had been jettisoned, replaced by the silver castings salvaged from the Wreck of the Ten Sail. Now that the new ballast was in place, the *Panther* was again trimmed properly and making good time. The men grinned and talked freely as they worked, knowing a part of the treasure hidden below belonged to them.

I was lost in thought recalling how I had come to be captain of this rabble. It was hard to believe it had only been three short years since Gasparilla, the infamous pirate, had taken the ship my family was on. I knew not the fate of my parents, but over time my bitterness and anger had diminished and I had fallen in love with the sea. I became his cabin boy and confidant and later escaped his demise with a small number of surviving crew and a good portion of the loot.

My thoughts drifted to Rory. How different it had been with her. Now that I knew the reason behind her constant questions and nagging I scolded myself for not having seen it earlier. Returning to England by whatever means available had been her only goal. I had thought I loved her, but, although I was voted captain by the crew and commanded this ship, I was only eighteen and had to admit my naivety in such matters.

One of the men called from the deck. I woke from my trance, moving to the edge of the spar for an unobstructed view. A cloud dead ahead hovered over a thin line of black on the water. Little Cayman. I looked further east and toward the starboard side and saw another cloud marking its sister, Cayman Brac. There we would anchor and repair the ship.

I could feel the boat respond to the change in course and held tight as the *Panther*, now close-hauled, bit into the waves. Passing the smaller island, we headed toward Brac. When its trees and beach were visible, I kissed Shayla and climbed down to the deck, shouting words of encouragement and praise to the men, calling any name of the freedmen that I remembered as I made my way to the helm.

"Where's Phillip?" I asked Swift, who was at the wheel. Shayla's father was a local and veteran of the sea. We needed him if we were going to avoid the treacherous reefs that ringed these islands.

"Sent Red below to find him," Swift answered.

A few minutes later, Red emerged with Phillip in tow and the two came toward the helm. When Rhames joined us, I found myself looking at the last remaining men from the *Floridablanca*.

"Is there an anchorage we can use here to repair the ship? Something away from the governor's eyes?" I asked Phillip.

"It's been thirty years since I've been to sea," he answered. "I don't remember much from my youth, but the traders described these islands well enough."

He put his hand to his brow to get his bearings. "The further island, Brac, is best. There's water on that one," he said.

That was good news. "And what of an anchorage?" I asked.

"If it were me, I'd stay offshore and do a bit of reconnaissance. Pirates have been known to use these islands to replenish their water and food stocks."

Pirates. The word grated on me. Since our escape we carried that brand at every turn. There was no washing the stink off. That was precisely why Pott, the man bound in our hold, was still alive. It was my intention to present him to the crown's man in Jamaica to testify to our innocence as well as alert the crown to the treachery of the governor of Grand Cayman. We had to do this before the governor made his own report incriminating us.

A Letter of Marque was my goal. The document would allow us to move about under the protection of the crown as privateers. Though privateers were a breed a bit too close to pirates for my liking, I intended to use the moniker to legitimize our crew, even though it would cost us half of our treasure. As far as I was concerned, half was better than nothing, and right now, without a place to spend it, that was all our treasure was worth.

The silver we had just recovered from the wreck was another matter. That could be melted, recast and sold.

"Right then. Mason, take the wheel and let's set a watch. Get the best eyes in the rigging and let's see if we have company."

Once the watch was set, I stayed by the wheel watching the approach. The smaller island was barely visible on the horizon now. We were close to the Brac and starting to circle her. The bluffs to the east were immediately visible. Well over one hundred feet, they were by far the highest landmark for miles. Waves crashed against their base and I was so distracted that I forgot what I supposed to be looking for.

"What do we want to do about that?" Mason asked, pointing to a mast poking up on the other side of the island.

I turned away from the scenery. A lone mast in such a barren section of water was not a good sign. Most merchants traveled in convoys. A single ship was likely a pirate or privateer.

"The repair can wait." I looked at the cloudless sky, estimating how long our barrels of water would last without rain. "We can reach Jamaica in a day if the wind holds. There's just enough fresh water for the passage."

We were past the bluff, heading east toward open water, when I saw the other ship's sails raise. I called the men to stations and sprang to the rigging. I climbed to the topsail, clinging to the sheets to get the best vantage point to evaluate the threat. Shayla was still on the spar where I had left her and I saw the fear in her eyes. I nodded across the open space, doing my best to reassure her. The bluffs that had fascinated me just a few minutes before now hindered my vision, and I waited for the ship to reappear.

The ship cleared the island under full sail. She was every bit our equal, though I could tell she was not in the best repair. We might have a chance at escape. The *Panther* was fast and her hull recently cleaned, but with our inexperienced crew I wasn't sure we could coax the last few knots from her.

I heard Mason call orders to the men and the ship responded. It would take a few minutes to see if we could distance ourselves or if we would have to turn and fight.

CHAPTER TWO

With full sails, we put enough distance to place us safely out of cannon range and I focused on the seas ahead. Rhames called the men back to their stations from the stern rail, where they were staring at the ship.

"What's with her sails?" one called out.

I turned to the stern and with the glass I could clearly see what they were talking about. She was poorly rigged and her sails were half black and half white. It was indeed a pirate ship. I had seen enough and climbed down to the deck.

"Pirates," I confirmed. "They've got to be in bad shape to be flying black sails during the day." It was a common ruse to use the soot-stained sails at night to avoid the reflection of the moon.

I looked to Rhames, Swift and Red, the last of Gasparilla's gang, and the expressions on their faces were pretty clear. They wanted to take her.

"Nick," Rhames started, just before I stared him down, wanting the respect of my position. He went quiet and waited.

Again the democracy of pirate crews was haunting me. Rhames would want a vote and I was certain I would be on the losing end. But as I looked back at the ship I knew what I needed to do.

"We take her!" I yelled.

A roar of approval came from the men on deck and I was immediately grateful for my instincts.

"Prepare the guns! Arm the men! Come about and set the course to take her on the starboard side," I yelled. The men cheered again and scrambled to their stations. I felt the sea change under my feet as the bow turned through the wind and the sails snapped over.

"Captain, if I may," Mason started.

Mason was my closest confidant and if it had come to a vote, I could usually count on him, but from his look I knew he disagreed now. The burly Georgian and I had spent many hours in conversation about the future and both agreed piracy in the Caribbean was at an end. I already suspected his opinion of my actions. "That ship'll come in handy," I said, lowering my voice so only he could hear.

"It's piracy," he said and spat on the deck.

"Is it piracy to take a pirate or a slaver?"

I wanted to remind him of the circumstance from which we had saved him. We had survived the interior of Florida and escaped the Everglades when we came upon the *Panther* anchored in the mouth of the Snake River on the west coast of Florida. Pirates had brought her there, seeking shelter in a storm. We took the ship and freed Mason from the hold. When we discovered him, several of his mates were already dead, lying next to him in their chains.

"I don't have to like it." He spat again.

"We could easily run, or we can put them out of business."

I turned to Swift and asked him to bring Pott, our prisoner, on deck. Pott's eyewitness report of the *Panther* taking a pirate ship would surely aid our cause.

The ships' paths were converging, and I saw a change come over the pirate ship. Where only seconds before she had seemed on her last leg, now her sails were trimmed to perfection and she was cutting a course not to evade us, but to confront us. Rhames saw it too.

"Foul play, the bastard," he exclaimed. "This is going to be more of a fight than we planned." He left me at the helm and went to the gunners, slapping backs and shouting encouragement as he worked his way down the line, checking placements and adjusting elevations.

Whatever was about to happen, I needed more information, so I took to the rigging. I was relieved that Shayla was still there but encouraged her to climb higher until the action was finished. If they intended to board us and take the ship, they would likely blast us with a round of grape aimed at the deck, and I wanted her safe from that and the small-arms fire that often preceded the grappling hooks. Unless the mast was taken down by a direct hit, it was the safest place aboard.

"It's a fight then?" she asked.

I didn't bother to answer. I glanced down at the deck and watched Rhames working frantically to instruct the crew leaders and arm the men. With the glass to my eye I studied our opponent. She was indeed ready for battle and we had badly underestimated her.

We were a quarter mile apart now, just enough sea room to jibe and steer wide of the ship, but I knew we had to fight. If she was indeed a better ship than we'd assumed, she would turn and chase us. Already I had seen her black sails come down one at a time, replaced by fine canvas. If we were to win her, we needed to take her on our own terms. I climbed down to direct the action.

Pott stood by the helm. "What's this piracy that you insist I witness?" he demanded.

I placed an arm around his shoulder and pointed a finger toward the pirate ship, now only a hundred yards away. "Mr. Pott," I told him, "that is a pirate, sir." I then called the order to prepare guns.

"Fire!" Rhames yelled, and silence prevailed for the interminable few seconds from when the flint struck the pan to the explosion from the barrel. There was a deafening boom and the *Panther* heeled to port. We rocked back, but there was too much smoke to see the result of our broadside.

"Set the hooks!" Rhames roared and threw the first grappling hook across the void to the other ship.

Two other hooks followed and the men worked in teams pulling the boats together. The first boarding party was perched on the rail ready to go when we took their broadside. At this range, their guns would be trained to fire solid balls at our hull and grape shot at the decks. They intended to sink us before we could board. It was a patient captain that would endure the first shot and wait for the hooks before firing.

"Go!" I called to the stunned crew. The fate of our own ship was out of our hands. "Mason, evaluate the damage."

I took the cutlass from the scabbard at my side and went for the rail. When I looked back, I saw Pott frozen like a statue by the wheel. I gave him a cavalier look I didn't feel and, bracing myself for the unknown, I jumped across the void, landing squarely on the deck of the pirate ship. The defenders backed away as several waves of our men swung across the divide, covered by the small-arms fire of the men remaining on our deck.

Hand-to-hand fighting was not my strong point, but I knew if I wanted to lead this ragtag group, I would need to be in front. Knowing my weakness for killing, Rhames and Red came to my side and took out two men each as we approached. Fortunately I never had to draw blood.

It was the sheer number of men that did it in the end. With the addition of the freed slaves to our crew, we outmanned the pirates two to one. Soon, the pirate crew was in a group around the mainmast with our men closing on all sides, the bloodlust clear in their eyes. I thought of Mason. Taking a pirate ship was one matter, the slaughter of her crew another. We were close enough to land that they could be put off in a longboat and have a chance at surviving.

I screamed for them to halt, but only a few heads turned. The deck was too loud. I attempted to push my way toward the mast, but the bulk of our crew was pushing closer as well. With no other option, I took the cutlass and slammed it into the rail, cutting the main sheet.

The sail bellowed and dropped, distracting everyone below as it fell to the deck. Instinct took hold of me and I grabbed the end of the line and held tight. The weight of the sail took me into the rigging and I found myself on the main yard. Below, there was confusion as our crew backed out from under the sail, leaving the pirates trapped underneath.

"Well done!" I yelled.

CHAPTER THREE

"Round them up and take an accounting," I yelled down to Rhames as our crew slowly peeled back the sail, ready to bind the men underneath. The situation on deck in hand, I glanced over at our ship to inspect the damage and saw Shayla twisted in the rigging.

She was caught in a mangled web of lines and wood. I panicked, thinking she was dead until I caught her eye. Sweat poured off her and she looked exhausted.

"Hang on!" I screamed and climbed down to the deck of the pirate ship. I left Rhames to the task of rounding up the pirates, a duty he relished. With three of the freedmen who I had observed to be comfortable in the rigging, we crossed to the *Panther*'s deck and started to climb.

The rigging was severely damaged and Shayla looked like she was spent and barely hanging on. The closer we got, the more precarious her situation appeared. The lines holding her were all damaged by the shot, their strands unraveling. Fortunately the rope ladder was intact and I was able to scurry up to her position, but when I arrived, I saw the spar was gone and I was unable to reach her.

With broken Spanish and hand motions I directed the men working their way towards her, commanding each to approach from a different angle so as not to put too much stress on any one line. We had her surrounded, but still couldn't reach her. I thought about using one of the loose lines to swing to her but was not sure if the remaining rigging would hold me. I looked down to see Blue watching us. With his weight being under one hundred pounds, he would have been perfect for the task, had it not been for his fear of heights.

I called to Shayla to hold on and slid down the outside lines of the ladder. My hands screamed in pain from the ropes, but I reached the deck in no time. Mason had already crossed from the pirate ship and was immediately by my side, staring up at Shayla and the mess above, shaking his head.

"We could rig a bosun's chair and send someone up. With a bit of luck, she could be cut out like that," he said.

I looked up and did not see how it would be possible to send a man in a chair into such a tangle of lines and wood, but there was no better idea and I trusted Mason's knowledge of ships. My train of thought was broken by a scream from the other deck, followed by a splash from something being thrown in the water. I looked for its source and saw that Rhames was demonstrating his own leadership style. It was nothing I could deal with for the moment. My focus was on Shayla.

Thunder rolled and, when I turned to look for its source, I saw that out of nowhere an anvil-shaped cloud with a black base had formed not a hundred feet from the water, reaching high into the sky. I had no doubt we were in for an intense storm and, unable to maneuver in our condition, we had to reach shelter before it swamped us. The storm could put us beam to the seas, where we were in danger of capsizing. It would mean working to get Shayla free while we were underway.

"Cut the ships loose," I commanded. "Phillip, have Rhames and Swift split the crew. They can take the pirate ship and follow us."

Phillip relayed my orders to Rhames and Swift, who set about splitting the freedmen into two equal groups. Rhames left the captives under guard with a threat that they would follow their friend over the rail if they caused any trouble. Then he started barking orders to the men to rig whatever canvas could hold wind.

Just as Phillip rejoined Mason and me at the helm, thunder boomed. Amidst the low rolling, there was a blinding flash of lightning, followed immediately by a sharp crash, and the storm was nearly upon us. We had been drifting and rolling with our beam to the gentle swells, but I knew that wind would come with the storm and the seas would increase. I had to get Shayla down before that. I left the navigation to Mason. He needed no orders and I could trust him to get the ships to the lee of the island before the storm hit.

I heard two lines snap and the ships separated. The hulls slammed together, but then separated. I left Rhames and Mason to their respective helms and focused my attention on the rigging.

"William, order the men to bring a pulley and line up from the hold and get the best climber to fasten it to the top of the mast." From that line I would follow Mason's advice and use a bosun's chair to go aloft. "We'll need some wood as well to fashion a boom," I added before I went to the hold to find our chair.

Haitian Gold

When I got back on deck, the motion of the ship had changed. We had the wind to our stern and a following sea, good conditions for now, but I suspected that would change. Over the port rail, I saw it closing; the leading edge bringing the wind would be on us in minutes.

Chair in hand, I climbed the rigging with abandon. Above me, men worked with the pulley and line, using what was left of a spar to extend the gear above where Shayla hung. I reached them and attached the canvas sling to the end of the line. Thunder boomed again and the men steadied me in the chair. We timed the swell and they pushed me free.

As comfortable as I was with heights, it was terrifying. Swinging freely a hundred feet above the deck, the slightest motion of the ship sent me flying several feet in either direction. Gradually, though, the men were able to lower me to the mess that held Shayla, and I was able to grab onto the twisted lines for support. With my dagger in my teeth, I sorted through the lines, judging which were critical to the ship, and went to work cutting the others.

The clouds were close enough to block the sun and I shivered when the first drops of rain hit my skin. Lightning flashed around me, but I forced myself to concentrate on the task at hand. It was tedious work, but one line at a time fell away, allowing me to get closer. A gust rocked the ship and I used its momentum to finally reach her. I grabbed ahold of Shayla and pulled her to me. We were face to face and I thought I saw a smile when the wall of water hit.

I was instantly blinded as the force of the waterspout plowed through us. Shayla dug her nails into my back, clinging for life, as we swung out over the ship until, with a loud snap that

15

sounded like a musket shot, the chair broke free and we fell for what felt like an eternity and smacked into the sea.

The force of the fall along with our combined weight drove us deep below the surface. I felt Shayla slash at me as she tried to free herself and I suddenly realized I had no idea if she could swim. I was close to panic. The canvas seat was wrapped around me, its line binding my legs. Shayla hit me again and I had no choice but to push her away. Neither of us had a chance if I drowned. With both feet still bound together I kicked like a dolphin toward the surface. My eyes stung from the salt, but I refused to close them; the sunlight filtering through the water provided my only hope. The weight of the rigging did its best to counter my efforts and soon my lungs were empty. I focused on the light above and I could see the ripples of water on the top. With renewed hope I kicked harder. The surface looked only feet away. Feeling the gag reflex that would end me, I kicked again, and suddenly my head broke through.

I tried to tread water until I could regain my strength, but our struggle was not yet over. The chair and line were still tight around me, pulling me onto my side and forcing seawater into my mouth. I was facedown and helpless when I felt a hand pull the line away and I was finally able to roll onto my back and breathe. Shayla surfaced beside me and we looked at each other as only two people who have faced death together can.

Once we caught our breath and were both free of the line, I spun in a circle looking for the ships. The storm had skirted past, but the seas were still white-capped from the wind. We crested a wave and I saw the masts. They had survived the storm and were limping under whatever sail they could muster toward the bluff rising from the island in the distance. There was no point in yelling, but we tried anyway, our smiles fading to worried looks as we realized we were on our own.

CHAPTER FOUR

Thankfully Shayla was a strong swimmer. We held hands and kicked on our backs, looking back every few minutes to check our course against the bluff—the only feature still visible over the waves. But despite our efforts we were drifting away from land.

"We're not going to make it, are we?" Shayla asked, spitting seawater from her mouth between words.

I tried not to show my concern. "Just hold on. The winds should die soon," I said, hoping it was true. The tail of the storm had just passed and the sky was now a brilliant blue. I would have liked to say more and reassure her, but the waves forced water into my mouth as well.

With each kick, I felt our energy wane, and I knew if something didn't happen soon we would succumb to the sea. I gritted my teeth and closed my eyes. When I opened them, I saw birds overhead. A flock of white seagulls swarmed the surface, crashing bait nearby while several larger frigate birds circled high overhead. It was the latter that caused me alarm for they were scouting the larger predators below the baitfish.

I wasn't sure if Shayla knew the significance of the birds. I said nothing. One of the frigates dove and crashed the surface not twenty feet from us, scattering the smaller birds working the surface. The large bird resurfaced and fluttered its wings, hovering inches over the cresting waves. I watched while it ate the small fish, expecting a fin to break the surface. I thought the bird would head skyward and join the flock, using the high winds to locate more baitfish. Instead, it settled on the surface. That's when I knew something was odd and kicked toward it.

The board was fresh in the water, and I guessed was from one of our ships. Shayla must have seen it too because we were both now kicking with everything we had left. Every so often a larger wave came along and pushed the board further out of reach, but finally we grabbed ahold of it, scaring off the bird, and pulled our upper bodies out of the water.

It was a long time before we talked. When my breath finally returned, I lifted myself higher out of the water and scanned our surroundings. The bluff, thankfully, didn't appear further off. In fact, we appeared to be floating toward it. In the time we had taken to reach the board, the storm winds had passed and the currents had changed.

Shayla recovered and saw the land, too. Together we lifted ourselves all the way onto the board, lay side by side and began kicking toward the bluff. Aided by the current, we gradually closed the gap.

***

We both yelled for the longboat ahead of us, but my throat burned from the salt water and my voice didn't carry. Even though we weren't sure they had seen us, we changed direction and headed toward the small craft. The current had other ideas, though, and started to pull us away. Just as we were about to give up and turn back, a man yelled and we saw the boat turn. Minutes later we were hauled aboard and collapsed exhausted against the gunwale.

"Thought we lost you there. That damn waterspout almost capsized us," Swift said in between barking orders to the half dozen freemen at the oars.

All I could do was nod while I caught my breath. I could feel Shayla shivering next to me and realized I was doing the same. We huddled together as the skiff cleared the bluff and entered a small anchorage in the lee of the island. Out of the wind, the seas settled and I took the opportunity to ask the questions I needed answered before we reached the ships.

"And what of the pirate ship?"

"She took some damage, but it was the *Panther* that took the brunt. She's going to need a new mainmast," he said.

"The pirates?" I asked.

"Still bound on the deck. A bit wetter than they would like," he laughed.

Shayla shivered again, and I pulled her closer. It was good news that Rhames had done nothing rash while I was gone. The pirate crew was a burden, but I would not have their blood on my hands.

"Looks like a battle-hardened lot. Maybe we can have them join," he said.

I had thought the same but had discarded the notion quickly. The last thing we needed was a dozen more pirates aboard. It was hard enough to control the three we already had. No, I thought. Better to put them ashore and leave them to fend for themselves.

We reached the *Panther* and Swift skillfully guided the longboat to the stern. Several heads appeared over the rail, each shouting encouragement to us as we climbed the rope ladder. Just behind Shayla, I reached the deck, where Mason embraced us. A cheer went up from the crew, followed a minute later by a similar chorus from our men on the pirate ship.

"Something's a bit odd with those two," Mason said.

I followed his glance to the pirate ship and saw Rhames and Red standing off to the side of the other cheering men. "We could use some dry clothes and food," I said, trying to downplay his concern. "Then we can talk." I turned and led Shayla past the crew and toward my cabin.

Mason followed us below and waited until Shayla had entered the cabin and closed the door before he spoke up. "Rhames and Red are strutting around like pirates over there. They might be up to something, Nick."

"It's just the thrill of the fight that's got into them," I said. He gave me one of his looks that said he knew more than I did and went back on deck.

Once I was inside with Shayla, we stripped off our wet clothes, and despite what we had just been through I couldn't help but be aroused by her naked body, though I knew my duties lay elsewhere.

I did not share Mason's fears, but I knew his judgment to be sound. Wanting to see for myself, I left Shayla and went topside. It was getting dark and there was little activity. In fact, the deck of the *Panther* was near empty. I found Mason by the helm, smoking a pipe and staring across the water at the pirate ship anchored a hundred feet away. The ship was lit and the drunken banter carried across the water.

"Sounds like they found some rum aboard," Mason said. "Quite the party. Maybe we ought to put an end to it."

I looked up at our shattered mast and even in the dim light I could see the damage to the rigging. "Maybe not a good idea right now. Let them drink their fill and they'll be easier to deal with tomorrow," I said.

A pistol fired, followed by a splash as cheers went up from the men. "Reckon that's the captain," Mason said, drawing on his pipe again, "and from the sound of it, they've already cut the men loose."

I suspected he was right and went to the rail to look at the ship. The pirate crew had me worried. If Rhames and the others wanted to return to their old ways, they now had the numbers.

"What do you make of it?" I asked him.

"Not sure, but I'll keep watch tonight. Still thinkin' we should put an end to it. Make sure the prisoners are safe," Mason said.

"Not till the liquor's gone. Let them drink their fill. Tomorrow is soon enough." Despite my worry, I had been through a lot with Rhames and his men, and Mason's concerns could keep for one night.

Tired of the conversation, I went to the rail. My eyes adjusted to the darkness and I could see the other ship's outline against the water. I studied her rigging, trying to evaluate the damage and plan for the repairs. Our broadside had crippled her as well. It would take many days to make both boats seaworthy again.

Just as I was about to turn away, a bright red light flashed in the sky. I turned and saw Rhames at the rail waving a pistol in the air. Two rockets exploded high in the sky. What was he doing? I did not want a confrontation now, but the flares could reveal our position.

"Stop with the rockets!" I shouted across the water. "You'll give away our position!" I regretted I couldn't do much to enforce discipline that night. Anything could happen when rum was involved, which explained the next rocket being pointed at me, but Rhames must have seen my reasoning. He turned the pistol away and I heard him shout to the men. When he disappeared, I could hear him leading the men in one of their pirate songs.

Mason was by my side now, staring at the other ship. "I'm not trusting of that lot," he said.

"Mason," I said, not taking my eyes off the other ship, "have you checked the hold?"

CHAPTER FIVE

Mason's fears were starting to register with me. I took a lantern and climbed down the ladder to the hold. Before I rested, I needed to set eyes on our treasure. The small light cast long flickering shadows against the walls as I made my way into the creaking darkness.

The chests were where we'd left them and looked untouched. I moved past them, crawled through the small passage to the fore compartment and lifted the hatch to the bilge. On my belly, I lowered the lantern into the dark space. The silver ballast was there as well. I breathed a sigh of relief and replaced the hatch when a noise startled me and I saw a figure huddled in the corner.

Unarmed, I approached cautiously. The figure was in the fetal position and as I got closer, I heard it moaning softly. I moved closer, holding the lantern in front of me.

It was Pott. He looked at me through bloodshot eyes, his face a mask of pain.

"What's wrong with you?" I asked.

He tried to lean forward but collapsed back onto the deck. In a moment of panic, I thought he was dead, but before I could reach out and touch him, he moved.

"I'm going to find Lucy. Maybe she can help you," I said and went for the ladder. I climbed to the deck and again heard the roar of the pirates across the water. With that new uncertainty, I could not afford to lose Pott and his testimony.

I had no idea where Lucy got her healing powers, but I knew firsthand from when the panther had attacked me in the backwoods of Florida that they were formidable. It had been hours now since I'd found Pott collapsed on the deck of the hold, and I could do nothing but sit back and watch while the pigmy healer worked feverishly to revive him. Under her breath, she chanted and cursed, both in languages that I couldn't understand, and I had a pang of anxiety every time she shook her head. Shayla came to her side, kneeling down, holding the lantern and helping whenever she could. For now, her earlier revulsion toward Pott was hidden.

From the height of the moon, I guessed it was well after midnight when I climbed onto the deck to fetch Lucy some water. It was quiet now. The only sound was the waves caressing the hull. I had been right not to stop the party. The silence told me I had at least until morning to figure things out. If Lucy could work her magic on Pott, I would have to call it a good night.

"Lucy says he will live," Shayla said, coming up beside me. "She pulled the most peculiar thing from his mouth I have ever seen."

"Good. We need his testimony," I said dismissively and went back to my thoughts.

She remained by me and we watched the other ship in silence. I was grateful for her company and thought of Rory, who would be questioning me about my intentions rather than offering me comfort. But my mind was still working, wondering what I would do on the morrow.

Mason's fears were not unfounded—they were, after all, pirates—but he had mistrusted Rhames, Red and Swift from the beginning. He seemed to ignore that Rhames had backed me as captain and had remained loyal to me, and I had rewarded that loyalty, our hold full of treasure and our ballast solid silver. Still, they were pirates and unpredictable. I would have to keep a weather eye.

I left Shayla at the rail, scooped a bucket of fresh water from the barrel by the mast and took it back to the hold. To my surprise, Pott was upright, leaning against the bulkhead. Lucy looked exhausted and was about to climb the ladder to the deck when I noticed something in her hand.

"What's that?" I asked, wincing at the smell as she moved toward me.

"Is the bad, Mr. Nick. He be better now. The evil is removed."

I leaned toward the rag she held open for my inspection and saw what looked like a mass surrounding a black tooth. Thankfully, she covered it up and climbed the ladder before I could gag. If that was what was causing him discomfort, I couldn't blame his foul mood.

I moved to Pott and extended a ladle of water to him. "How are you?" I asked, as he drank eagerly and finally smiled.

"The woman is a miracle. I don't know if it was the work of God or the spirits she called, but I am healed," he said. "Where are we? The last I remember was the cannon fire."

"Off the small island. We captured the pirate ship and her

crew."

"Thought we were headed for Jamaica for me to give a statement."

"Things change. Both ships are in need of repair," I said.

I waited for him to drink his fill before questioning him further. I was starting to worry about the governor. Were it not for the battle with the pirate ship we would be in Jamaica by now, but our ships were crippled and only a day's sail from Grand Cayman. These barren islands were still within his jurisdiction. I had only a few hours to figure out a plan before the men started to rise. From my experience with Gasparilla's band, a hungover crew was as dangerous as a drunken one.

Finally, Pott placed a hand up signaling that he'd had enough. I put the ladle back in the bucket and continued my questioning.

"So tell me, what do you figure the governor's next move will be?" I could only hope that he knew the mind of my adversary after being his right-hand man for so many years.

He thought for a moment. "I don't expect him to lick his wounds for long." He rubbed his mouth where the abscess had been removed and smiled. "If I was him, I'd run to Jamaica as fast as I could and try and beat you to the local governor. Could be you'll be all right here. It's a ways from him, and without a real fleet he can't chase you everywhere."

I knew he was probably right and relaxed slightly. Even though these atolls were part of the Cayman territory, they were seventy miles from the larger island, where the governor was based.

"So you think we could hole up here and make repairs?" I asked.

"Seems you don't have much choice," he said.

He looked better and I extended an arm to help him to his feet. "Go on up and get some food. Most of the crew are sleeping off the rum they found. If I were you, I'd take to the cabin before they wake. They don't trust you and it won't help to be showing your face." The governor had placed Pott and his sidekick on the *Panther* to oversee the recovery of the treasure. I knew the man to be shrewd, and despite his initial animosity, I had lobbied to save his life in exchange for his testimony. As for the sidekick, Rhames had dispatched him.

Pott nodded in understanding. "Please extend my thanks to the woman," he said and moved toward the ladder.

"You can extend your gratitude by your testimony to the governor in Jamaica."

"I'll do that, but what are your plans for me after that?" he asked.

"We'll see," I answered.

***

With sleep eluding me, I relieved the freedman and stayed on deck to watch the sunrise. In the dawn's light, the pirate ship came into view and I studied her lines, surveying what damage our cannon had done to her. With her crew asleep and rigging in tatters, she had the feel of a ghost ship, but she would be repaired in a few days if there was no structural damage. The *Panther* was in worse condition. She needed a new mast. Between the two ships, we might be able to make one seaworthy vessel, but I wanted both.

I turned to the island behind me and studied the shoreline. The outline of several large pine trees was visible in the growing light and I hoped one might be suitable for a new mast, but I would wait for Mason. He was the only man we had whom I trusted in such matters. A work schedule formed in my head and I was about to go below to write it down when I heard the first sign of activity from the pirate ship.

Blue must have heard it too. He came beside me and we watched the ship together.

"Men be mad," he said.

Mason appeared next to us. "Careful, they're likely to be in a fighting mood," he cautioned as I climbed down the ladder to the skiff.

I rowed the skiff over to the pirate ship, tied the painter to the ladder and climbed onto the deck. Most of the men lay prone, having dropped where the alcohol had left them. Several were sitting up, rubbing their eyes. I moved through the group, thankful to see the previous occupants of the ship still tied around the mainmast. At least I only had three pirates to deal with. Finally I found Rhames near the forepeak.

"Rhames," I said, touching his shoulder.

"Aye, Nick," he said, lifting an eyebrow and slowly raising himself up onto one elbow.

"We need to talk," I said.

"Aye, we do," he replied, rubbing his eyes and starting to rise. "The boys and I have some ideas."

I tried not to react, but this was what I'd been afraid of. The three remaining men from Gasparilla's crew were pirates at heart and I suspected they knew no other way. The thought of becoming legitimate was foreign to them.

"All right," I responded. "Get them together."

Rhames rose slowly and stumbled before he gained his

footing and staggered toward the stern. As I waited, I worked my way among the men on deck, acknowledging as many as I had names for. I only had a few minutes before the fate of my command was decided and I needed the support of every man I could rouse. Rhames joined me back at the helm, followed by Swift and Red, shaking the cobwebs from their heads.

"We've been talking about taking this ship, splitting the loot and getting on with it," Rhames said slowly.

I remained silent, both to give him some discomfort and to allow myself time to craft a reply. Splitting the treasure and ships was indeed a fair end to our relationship, but I knew that sooner rather than later he would be caught. Rhames, like most pirates, lived for the moment and had not the care or forethought to plan for the future. Besides, I had no doubt that, if they were captured, Red and Swift would turn on me in exchange for their lives. I needed to take control.

"I thought the idea of amnesty appealed to you?" I asked. "It'll take a few days to get the ships seaworthy, but after that we'll make Jamaica in two days. It'll be a small matter to have the governor's man give his testimony."

"You think that's going to work?" He spat over the rail. "They'll see us for what we are the minute that sorry clerk is alone with them. He'll say whatever they want to hear."

I hadn't thought about Pott betraying us, especially after what Lucy had just done for him.

"Leave Pott to me. He's making noise like he wants to join us. Lucy pulled some foul thing from his mouth last night and—"

"He'll harbor a grudge against me for killing his man," Rhames said, cutting me off before he spat again.

"All the same, we can be a powerful force if we stay

together."

"A force of what?" he asked. "That's the problem with this treasure hunting idea of yours. Where do we go? At least with pirating, the decisions are easy."

I searched for an argument, but his mind seemed made up. With half the treasure and a ship, we would have find a place to hide the treasure. We would be vulnerable without the pirates. Mason was a good navigator and experienced salvage man, but lacked the shrewdness that came with the pirate mindset. Having Rhames, Red and Swift gave us a military advantage, and after all we'd been through I had come to trust and like the men. I needed a ploy to delay the vote.

CHAPTER SIX

"I've a right to go through the captain's log and papers before we part ways," I said.

Rhames looked at Swift and Red and the two pirates shrugged. "Aye, that is your right," Rhames said before leaving me to wake the rest of the crew.

Only slightly relieved, I entered the captain's cabin and looked at the mess surrounding me. Logbooks and charts were scattered about the small room, and the smell of rum was strong, with empty bottles laying on the table and floor. It would take longer than I'd thought to sort this out, but any delay was good. I moved the bottles to the side and opened a porthole.

The fresh air snapped my mind back to the task and I started sorting the logbooks and charts, perusing each one, keeping an eye out for handwritten notes. I noticed several different styles of writing in the margins and thought these must have come from the ships the pirates had taken. Rhames and his men couldn't read, so the logbooks would be of no use to them, but they understood the value of the charts and would never let them leave the ship. Still, I sorted the charts by language and soon had small piles of English and French. I couldn't help but notice the French charts were all in the same hand and very detailed, but there was no French logbook to go with them. All of the logbooks were in English.

I began my search for the missing logbooks when I heard someone at the door and turned to see William, one of the freedmen, in the entry.

"Rhames says to tell you we haven't got all day," he said. "He intends to be underway before dark. He's happy to send some men to split the treasure."

"I'll only be a few more minutes. Just looking for the log." I glanced at the charts and looked back at William. "You can read French, right?"

"My duties require me to read and write in several languages," he said.

I needed him.

"Please tell Rhames I'm working as fast as I can. Then come back and see if you can lend your eye to these."

While I waited for William to return, I searched the cabin. The French logbooks had to be here and I was intent on finding them before Rhames ran out of patience. Rather than keeping order, I started tossing everything, working from one corner of the small cabin to the other. I found several pistols and a small chest, but no logs. I smiled when I found a bound book under a false panel in the captain's chest, but on inspecting it, I noticed it was barely maintained. The pages held only scant details, nothing like the carefully written notes and diagrams on the charts. It was a decoy. The real log would be hidden better.

Finally I reached the bunk and tossed the mattress to the deck. Nothing. I was about to give up when I saw what looked like knife marks marring the edge of one of the boards making up the pallet. With my dagger, I pried the corners of the board and it came loose, but before I could see what the cavity held, Rhames appeared at the door. I sat on the bunk with my heart beating loudly in my chest, trying to hide my find. While he surveyed the disarray of the cabin, I thought how only the day before I would have readily shared this all with him.

"Find what you're looking for yet?" he asked. "The men are getting restless."

"There's a chest of coin and some pistols there," I offered, pointing to the chest.

Rhames took a step forward, and at first I thought he was making a move for me and regretted not taking a pistol for myself, but he turned and went for the chest.

"I haven't found the key," I said.

"No worries there," he said, stowing the chest under one arm.

He left without a word and I knew I had some time. The chest looked substantial and I expected it would take some effort to open it. Besides, his greed would keep him at the task until it was complete.

A moment later, William stood in the door and I motioned him to the pile of French charts on the table. While he examined them, I got up and stuck my hand through the open board. There were several books in the compartment and I soon understood why there was such an effort to keep them secret. They were the records from the ships the pirates had taken. There were five of them and I paged through them until I found the one with the distinctive handwriting of the Frenchman.

Opening the French log, I saw the detail I knew was missing

from the fake book. Though I couldn't understand them, the notes were meticulous and the diagrams skillfully drawn. With the book, I went to William, who was studying the charts on the deep windowsill, where the light was better.

I glanced over his shoulder at the chart spread before him. "Can you make anything out?" I asked.

"Much about Haiti," he said. "There's more to it than is marked here, though."

I placed the logbook in front of him. "Maybe this will help."

He caressed the leather-bound cover and looked at me. "We need a place to talk."

I was intrigued but still hesitant to take anything. There was no telling the state of mind of the men after drinking the night before. "Do you need the charts or will the logbook suffice?"

"There's a mystery here. I think it will take both to find out what it is."

I heard activity on deck and figured we had little time. Haiti was not a place I would go willingly, but if there was a mystery in this part of the world, that meant there was treasure and that held my attention. The Frenchman's handwriting made it clear that he was an educated man, and such a man would not chase a small treasure.

I needed to see what Rhames was up to. "Keep reading," I instructed William and left the cabin.

The men were on their knees around the strongbox. Its lid was scarred and the lock dented from their attempts to open it. "Tough bugger," I said. A chill went up my spine when they all turned to stare at me. "Might have seen a key in the cabin. I'll be right back."

"Hide the chart in the book," I told William while I feigned a search for the key. I hadn't seen one, but as I pretended to look, an idea occurred to me. I went back to the bunk and stuck my hand in the hole, and, sure enough, far back in the corner my finger struck metal. I reached further in and extracted a ring with a dozen keys. "Hurry," I told William and went back on deck.

"Here. I'm betting it's one of these." I tossed the ring to Rhames, who grabbed it from the air and went to work on the lock. I was hoping it would take longer, but almost immediately one of the keys fit and Rhames gave me a queer look as he turned the lock. "It's part mine too," I said, standing my ground. Rhames grunted and lifted the lid.

Jaws dropped but no sound came from the crews mouths as sunlight hit the gold bar Rhames held over his head. I had seen a lot of treasure over the years, but nothing like this. The bar was larger than his hand and clearly heavy. The circle tightened, each man eager for a closer look.

"Get back, you bastards," Rhames called out and set the bar back in the chest.

He retreated slightly and allowed me to inspect the piece. I lifted the bar from the chest and turned it in my hands. After my years with Gasparilla, I knew what to look for. The gold was pure, with no sign of slag or impurities. But it was not the value of the gold that intrigued me. It was where it had come from. If someone had gone to the trouble to cast a bar this size, there must be more. I held the piece to the light, looking for any stamps or engravings on it, and noticed a small mark on the bottom.

Wanting to make the find seem insignificant, I placed the bar back in the chest, turned away without comment and looked at the faces of the crew, trying to get a feel for how to play this. From the corner of my eye I saw William emerge from the companionway with the logbook under his arm. Every eye was on the chest and no one noticed him move to the stern. I was watching him as best I could to see if he was able to get off the ship when he stopped short of the ladder.

"Sails!" he yelled and retreated from the rail.

I only had to climb a few feet into the rigging to make out the tip of a mast on the horizon.

CHAPTER SEVEN

"Frigate!" I yelled and jumped down to the deck.

Rhames and I exchanged looks. Our negotiation would have to wait. I looked toward the horizon, but the bluffs blocked the view of the ship. Not wanting to suffer the same fate as the day before, I carefully navigated the mess of tangled lines and spars hanging from the mast. Halfway up, I saw it.

"She's flying the Union Jack," I yelled down to Rhames.

"She seen us?" Rhames called back.

The warship was still too far away to see if her gunports were open, but I studied her course. "If she hasn't, she soon will." The only frigate in these waters was under control of the governor and I suspected her watch had seen the rockets the night before. Fortunately we were in the lee of the island and the frigate would have to circle around it before it could reach us.

There was no point in staring at it. I ordered two of the men to keep watch and climbed down to the deck. The men, still bleary-eyed from the night before, aware of the threat, were now on their feet and awaiting orders.

I called for our depth and heard two fathoms called from the bow. "I'm not sure if we're not better staying in the shallows," I said to Rhames, Swift and Red, who were standing around me.

"But she'll blast us to high hell if we just sit here," Rhames argued.

He was right. We were in a bad spot.

"We can't run, and there's not enough shallow water to hide in," I said.

"The treasure's on the *Panther*. We could sacrifice this ship and try and save her," Red said.

Rhames glared at him and Red grew silent.

The thought had crossed my mind. We could turn the ship into a pyre and send it toward the frigate, but it would have to make a direct hit, or else the frigate would evade it. The ploy might buy us some time, but the *Panther* was badly crippled and could not outrun the larger ship. We needed to even the score.

"Check the powder stores," I ordered Swift, then I called across the rail for Mason to come join us. An idea was forming in my head and it would take the coordination of both ships to pull it off. "How much time do you reckon we have?" I asked Rhames.

"She's going to have to tack at least twice to get around the island," Rhames calculated. "I'd say an hour until we're in range of her cannon."

"But she won't open fire," I said, "not with the treasure aboard."

"Aye. But there's not much to stop her from setting up a broadside and holding us at bay while she boards. We're sitting ducks," Rhames explained.

Mason was in the skiff and almost to us. I tried to read my opponents' mind while we waited. If they were not intent on sinking us, and with us sitting so close to land, they had few choices as to how to keep us under their guns. The frigate was approaching from the southwest. There was little doubt of her course and I estimated where she would make her move.

Mason came aboard and I laid out our situation. "We can't run and we don't have the firepower to match her," I said.

"Got five kegs of powder," Swift interrupted.

"See what you can find for flints and pans," I ordered.

"What are you thinking?" Rhames asked.

"They want the *Panther*, right?" The men nodded and I told them my plan. Despite their puzzled expressions, no one questioned my authority.

The forepeak of the frigate was just visible now as she rounded the island and we knew we had little time. Swift and several men hauled the barrels of powder onto the deck and lined them up along the rail. Rhames, with a skeptical look on his face, was busy removing the firing mechanism from several pistols while keeping one eye on the horizon. Mason split the crew and had half a dozen men cut loose sections of line from the damaged rigging and drop them to the deck, where several others waited to tie the lengths together. The other half of the crew focused on making the ship seaworthy. For my plan to work, we would need the frigate to think both of our ships were making a run for it.

Rhames took the firing mechanisms and hammered one into each barrel, while several men coated them with pitch and lard. I looked over the rail. The frigate had rounded the point, tacked again and was closing. I guessed she would have to come about twice more to get within range of us, but our decks were now visible and she could see everything we did.

"You're sure about this?" Rhames asked. "Maybe we should cut the pirates loose and have them fight with us."

I shook my head. We were outnumbered by the crew of the frigate. They were better armed and were trained to fight together. "If they board us, it'll be a bloodbath with or without the extra men," I responded.

"Ready here," someone called down from the rigging.

I looked up and inspected their work. The foremast was cleared of debris and had its main and topsail ready. It would have to be enough. The mainmast was still in shambles.

Mason was at the ladder, ready to return to the *Panther* with the end of the rope we had fashioned. "You coming?" he asked.

"Best stay here," I said, tying the other end to the rail. "There's not a leader in this bunch."

"Watch your back, then," he said and dropped out of sight to the waiting skiff.

I watched the rope uncoil from the deck, trailing behind the small boat to the *Panther*.

I turned back to Rhames. He had the barrels lined up along the rail. A section of cargo net encased each one, with a rope loop waiting to attach it to the main line. Mason had reached the *Panther* and I turned to watch the frigate, waiting for her to come about. That brief second would give us the cover we needed. Her course changed slightly, and as she turned into the wind, I waited for her sails to luff. Slowly the wind left her sails and I saw the booms swing. We had the cover we needed. I gave the signal.

Rhames tied the first keg to the line. I winced as it splashed, hoping it would need something harder than the water to trigger the mechanism. Every fifty feet he attached another barrel.

Once they were over the rail, I watched the four bombs bobbing in the water and realized how difficult this would be. For there to be any chance of the frigate's hull striking the firing mechanism and setting off the charge, we would have to lure her between our ships, a distance of only a few hundred feet. The only thing in our favor was that with the size of the charges, it would take only one to disable her.

The frigate was bearing down on us. It was time. I looked over at the *Panther*. Mason was driving the crew hard to rig whatever canvas the broken masts could handle. I called to raise anchor. The pirate ship would have to drag the *Panther* until she was ready.

The anchor chain came aboard and Rhames took the helm. He called for the sails to be raised and I went to the stern rail. The ship started to make headway and I watched the rope stretch in the water. It snapped taut and I held my breath, not knowing if it would hold or maybe trigger one of the explosives.

Mason had managed to get a sail up and pressure came off the line as he eased the *Panther* along the same course. Our two boats were now a hundred yards apart, with the pirate ship slightly ahead. The illusion of the two ships escaping appeared perfect, but we would have to wait to see if the captain of the frigate would see our trap.

The four kegs were underwater, their wake all that was visible to the naked eye. I looked back. Mason followed slightly behind and inland of us, and the frigate was gaining on us quickly, her course running right between the two ships. The captain was not committing to either vessel until he got closer.

"Should just be a minute now," Rhames said from the helm.

The frigate was close enough to hear the gunports open and the scrape of the cannon being dragged forward on their carriages. I looked behind and saw they had both their port and starboard guns ready. He intended to take both of us. Now it was a waiting game to see if the captain of the frigate could fire his broadsides before his ship struck a keg.

All eyes were on the frigate. We were defenseless against a ship more than twice our size and built for war. I thought about releasing the lines and letting the kegs drift aft, but decided against it, unsure what the current would do with them. That's when I saw the flaw in my plan.

The forepeak of the frigate was at our stern, midway between our two ships, when I realized I had failed to take into account the momentum needed to set off one of the flintlock mechanisms. With both ships moving forward, it was not going to be enough to set off the charge.

I ran to the mainmast, grabbed the fire ax and made my way past open-jawed men to the starboard rail, where I waved the blade over my head, motioning for the other ship to cut the line. One of the men must have told Mason, because seconds later one of the freemen stood by the line with an ax in his hand. I raised mine over my head, watching him do the same. Then, in a single motion, we slammed the steel heads into the line.

The line snapped and vanished overboard. I watched the munitions drift back toward the frigate and held my breath.

The forepeak of the frigate was almost amidships, and I clearly heard the order from her captain to fire. Our crew heard it as well and hit the deck. We heard the roar of her bow chasers as they attempted to disable us. Shot smashed through the rail and men screamed. Next came the call to ready the hooks. They were preparing to board us. I was about to give up and prepare a defense when I heard it.

A thump came from underwater. Spray shot up and I heard the sound of wood splintering. Another keg exploded and I ran to the rail to see the damage. As we gazed at the huge hole in the frigate's bow, the mood of the ship changed instantly.

An eerie silence came over the frigate.

"We're taking on water," someone shouted. We were close enough to hear the order to abandon the attack and man the pumps. The ship had already fallen behind and was floundering, with two giant holes in her hull. I heard an order for her to come about, but it was too late. Her hull was already vanishing, bow first, into the sea. With her sails still raised, her momentum was driving her underwater. It happened faster than I'd thought possible. Amid the panic, several men jumped over the rail, and within seconds the frigate was gone, a large whirlpool marking the spot where she had vanished.

CHAPTER EIGHT

There was a long moment of silence and then a loud cheer erupted from both ships. Even the captured pirate crew joined in the celebration. The men slapped me on the back, congratulating me on our victory. It was no small matter for two crippled ships to take down a frigate.

"That was well done," Rhames said as I approached the helm.

I, along with the crew, was exuberant, but I couldn't let the moment go to waste. "Maybe we should reconsider parting ways," I said.

I knew Rhames would return soon enough to his earlier demands, but I did not want to split the treasure and crew. Without the pirate contingent we would be worthless in battle and prone to becoming a victim of the high seas. Without waiting for a response, I looked Rhames square in the eye and made my case.

"At least don't be rash about it," I continued. "The governor has no way of knowing what just happened and will assume the frigate is still out searching for us. We can use the opportunity to repair the boats and agree on a path. I'd even agree to offering the captives a place in the crew, with conditions, of course." The words came out better than I'd expected. As for the pirate crew, they had seen too much and I didn't have the stomach to put them to death.

Rhames rubbed the stubble on his chin and I could tell he missed the braided beard he'd worn as a pirate. "Aye, something to think on. I'll talk with the men later."

I was thankful for the reprieve. It would take both crews to step a new mast on the *Panther*. I looked back to where the frigate had gone down, and all I could see was some flotsam on the surface. There was no sign of longboats or survivors. A tinge of regret clouded my mind as I thought about how many men had likely gone down with the ship, but we'd had no choice. Still, it would be seen as an act of piracy.

I looked at the damage the bow-chasers had caused and saw several men down. I called four men over to haul our casualties to the rail, but when I approached and took a closer look, I was filled with remorse. William lay sprawled in a pool of his blood, his entrails spilled onto the deck. In his hands, he still clutched the logbook.

"Circle back to the island near the bluff," I instructed Rhames. "It's a good anchorage and there are trees there we could use to fashion a mast." Rhames nodded and I went to the rail and yelled for Mason to follow with the *Panther*. "I'll be below," I said and left the helm with the logbook under my arm.

It was dim in the captain's cabin and I realized that in my earlier haste I had left the loose plank out of place. I scolded myself for being careless, but everything remained as I had left it. I took one of the two lanterns hanging from the low ceiling, lit it, and brought it to the bunk to get one last look at the cavity within. I found nothing more and replaced the loose board and mattress.

The charts and logbooks were scattered on the table. I sat down with the lantern and started reading the English ones. The French log would have to wait until I could find another translator. I heard the anchor chain scrape against the hull and splash, then felt the ship change position when the hook grabbed. I remained studying the books, having to refill the lantern twice before I finished. It had consumed much of the night, but the work needed to be done. The logs contained firsthand information unavailable elsewhere. I committed the most valuable passages to memory, and anything secondary, I marked with torn pieces of paper. Once done, I pulled out the Frenchman's book and chart and lay them in front of me. I stared with tired eyes, the words eluding me. Finally, I closed the bloodstained book and left the cabin.

Swift was on watch and, after a brief exchange about the sinking of the frigate, I looked over at the *Panther*, outlined in the moonlight, the glow from a pipe visible on deck. Assured the watch was vigilant, I went and sat by the gunwale and rested my head against the rail.

***

It was light out when I woke, and the dryness of my eyes told me I hadn't slept enough. Still, there was no choice in the matter, and I rose. We needed to repair the boats, and quickly. The sooner we were able to escape the reach of the governor, the safer I would feel. Several tasks needed to be attended to, though, and I headed straight to the ladder and down to the skiff. I had stayed on the pirate ship overnight to keep an eye on things and wanted to see Shayla and speak to Mason before again confronting Rhames.

I inspected both ships from the skiff, and thought again about just how lucky we had been with the frigate. We wouldn't be so lucky the next time, and once the governor learned of the sinking, he would surely stop at nothing to find us. I rowed across to the *Panther*, and looking at her lines from this vantage point, the thought occurred to me to disguise her. With all the work she needed, a new cut to her sails would be a fairly easy addition.

All thoughts of work left me when I saw Shayla stretched out on the bunk. She pulled the light cover back to reveal her naked body and I couldn't resist her. We collapsed into each other's arms and it took well into the morning to spend our built-up passion. Later, lying in each other's arms, I explained my plans.

"Partner with Rhames?" she asked. "He worries me, always wanting to pirate." She paused. "And I don't like the way he looks at me."

I agreed with her assessment but still made my case. "We are safer with him than without him. With two ships, we are stronger and no one knows weapons and battle better than him."

She nodded a reluctant acceptance and we got up to get dressed.

Just as I was tying my boots, Shayla spoke up. "Maybe if I had a share he would respect me."

Giving a share to the woman of the captain was tricky business. The pirates, although not formally educated, were shrewd and knew politics. With her, Phillip, Mason and me, we would outvote them. This would not be lost on them. For now,

I did my best to satisfy her.

"I'll try," I said. "I'm going over to talk to them. I'll signal when I'm ready for you to come over with your father and Mason."

I rowed over to the pirate ship and climbed the ladder to the deck. Taking our group together would alert Rhames about my intentions. I gained the deck and started an inspection of the ship. Seeing that the decks were clear and repairs were already underway, it was evident that the rum had been consumed.

Red was on watch and I took over for him, with orders to rouse Rhames and Swift. I went back to the rail and signaled to Mason that I was ready. An hour later we were gathered by the stern rail. The governing body consisted of anyone with more than a full share and included Rhames, Red, Swift, Mason, Phillip and myself. Once we had decided on a plan, we would put it to a full vote. The three pirates looked over at Shayla.

"Not the girl," Rhames said.

I whispered to her to wait by the rail and she stalked away. The crew sensed something was afoot and started to close around us, but Red and Swift glared at any man who attempted to come within earshot.

"Show them the bar," I said. I wanted to set the stage.

Rhames reluctantly brought the chest from below and showed Mason and Phillip the gold bar. Stunned, they simply stared at it. I had seen it before, but stood likewise entranced. Just as Rhames set it back in the chest, I again saw the small engraving on the bottom. I knew I would have to set aside my curiosity to examine it at a later time.

The chest was locked away and we got down to the business of refitting the ships. Work crews were agreed upon, with

Mason heading the selection and fashioning of a new mast for the *Panther*. Rhames suggested an armed party search both islands for survivors of the frigate, and we agreed that any found would be captured, not killed.

With the easy decisions out of the way, I brought up my concerns. "And what of the pirate crew?" I asked the group.

They all looked at me. I knew Rhames wanted the pirates voted in to enhance his standing, but I had thought carefully about it. We needed men to man both ships and slaughtering them was out of the question. I had taken count of the freedmen and knew I still held a majority of the crew if the pirates chose to band together.

"And Shayla. Surely she deserves a stake," I added.

As expected, Rhames was the first to speak. "We can't very well release them and have them tell their tale," he said. "I vote they join with a full share each."

"I agree, but we lock the weapons at all times." I paused. "And the matter of the girl?" I hoped Rhames would be happy with the pirates being included and compromise on Shayla.

The others stood silent with their heads down. Finally Rhames spoke. "She's your woman and not part of the crew. I vote no."

Without exception, the others nodded their agreement and I turned to Shayla and shook my head. With a furious look on her face, she turned and jumped over the rail. I went after her and saw her swimming for the other ship. I was about to follow, but it would show weakness, so I remained with the crew.

Rhames called the men together and we moved to the starboard rail. The *Panther* lay at anchor less than a hundred feet away, her crew gathered on the port side within earshot.

Rhames relayed our plan and issued orders for the work parties. Everyone soon dispersed to their duties, leaving the two of us alone.

"We agree to leave any decision on splitting until the repairs are made and both ships are seaworthy," I said.

"Aye," he said.

I left him to his work and returned to the *Panther* with Mason and Phillip. I saw Phillip's concern as he scanned the deck for Shayla.

"She'll be all right," I said. "I'll talk to her." In truth, I wanted to avoid her until she cooled down.

Once on deck, Mason pulled me aside after he had given orders to the crew. "I don't trust those men, but I fear you're right and we need them. With that kind of treasure aboard, two ships and a fighting contingent will surely come in handy."

He had finally come around to my position, and I tried to keep the smile off my face. I needed a way to keep Rhames and his crew occupied. "We'll have to find us an adventure then."

***

I asked the freedman at the helm if he had seen Shayla. He assured me that she was safe below. I put her from my mind and turned to my next task—Pott.

I found him near the forepeak and thought I saw him smile. "You look to be better," I said.

"The woman has the gift. The pain has plagued me for years and now it's gone. I owe her."

"And what of us?" He looked queerly at me, and I decided with a man of his intelligence it would be better to lay it all out. "You saw us sink the frigate."

He stayed silent for a moment, staring at the deck. It was unsettling awaiting the judgment from the only man with the authority to clear us.

"Don't expect they were here to parlay," he said and looked me in the eye.

"So, you have no further loyalty to the governor?"

Again he stared at me and just shook his head.

"To tell you the truth, I don't care for that bastard Bodden. I was under his thumb for too long. Gruber, the one your man killed, was under orders from Bodden to watch me as well."

This was a surprising change in demeanor. Still, I wanted nothing left open to his machinations. "Let's be clear here," I started. "You are willing to denounce the governor and give testimony on our behalf."

"I am. And I'll be looking for employment as well. Don't expect I'll be offered another posting in his majesty's government after this."

I eyed him carefully and decided he was being truthful. "A position with the crew?"

He smiled. "I've always dreamed of a life at sea," he said almost boyishly.

We needed his support, but instead of agreeing right away, I chose to delay just to be sure he was sincere. "I'll put it to the men," I said and walked away. I wasn't sure if I could sell them on Pott's worth, but a man of his intelligence, his cunning and his knowledge of the government could prove to be invaluable.

I looked around, making sure everything was in order before turning to the companionway. With the logbook secured under my arm, I went to the cabin to see where I stood with Shayla.

CHAPTER NINE

I stood warily in front of the cabin door, steeling myself for the confrontation. Finally I summoned the courage to try the knob and found it locked from the inside. Despite my pleas, there was no answer when I called to her. It was a warm night, but I felt a chill deep in my bones and it was then that I knew what Shayla meant to me. One way or another, I had to rectify the situation, but with Rhames and the pirates voting against her, I had to tread carefully and be patient. I had sought for a way to placate her, but with the door locked, that would have to wait, too. The loss of her affection stung. I returned to the deck, hoping the night would change her mind.

The dogwatch had been mine, but my mind was churning, so when Red came on deck at two, I sent him back to his bunk. If I was not to get any sleep, I might as well allow him his. The sun was breaking through the thin layer of clouds on the horizon, stretching its fiery tentacles towards the sky, and I sniffed the air for any sign of bad weather.

With the dawn, men started moving around on deck. I tried to put Shayla from my mind and start planning the day. We would need to work quickly if weather was indeed on the way.

"Rough night?" Mason asked as he came up beside me.

"I've had worse," I replied stoically. "We ought to get the longboats in the water before the weather hits." He glanced to the sky and I could see he agreed with my concern.

"Best get the rigging squared away," he said.

I looked up at the tangled web of spars and lines. "You think you'll find what you need ashore?" I asked him. "I don't see any trees the size of a mast."

"I had a look with the glass yesterday and checked the stores in the hold. The other ship has the hardware to make the scarf joints we need to splice smaller bits together."

This was indeed good news. Instead of having to find and shape one large tree into a mast, we could use several smaller pieces and join them together.

Mason left to rouse the crew, and less than an hour later, the men were fed and divided into work parties. The skiff from the *Panther* and the longboat from the pirate ship were both loaded for their respective duties. The skiff, led by Rhames, was packed with half a dozen men, all heavily armed. Their duty was to scour the island for any survivors. I had seen several men jump from the frigate before she vanished, and if they were still alive they would need to be found. The larger longboat carried a score of men and all the tools we could find to aid them in cutting the trees needed for the mast. I watched until they landed on the beach and started my own work.

With most of the men aboard the pirate ship, there would be room on the *Panther*'s deck for the women to mend the sails. I called for Lucy and sent a party into the rigging. Soon the torn canvas fell to the deck. Lucy was already on deck sorting through the sails when Shayla appeared. The two women spoke and started working together. It felt like a dagger stabbing me when Shayla's glance passed over me without any sign of recognition.

There was no point spending too much time on the *Panther* until Mason had stepped the new mast. With the two smaller boats gone, we rigged a line and a makeshift raft to shuttle men and materials between the ships. I climbed down the ladder, set my feet on the rough wooden planks and, hand over hand, pulled the raft to the pirate ship, where I jumped onto the ladder and climbed to the deck. I was glad for the separation from Shayla.

The ship had been obviously jury-rigged, and I ordered all the sails and line taken down. The canvas was piled on the foredeck, out of the way, until the women were able to inspect and repair it. Next I had the men cut down all the lines while I climbed into the rigging myself and inspected the spars, ordering those that were not right to be removed. The masts were near bare when we finished.

By noon, the spars that could be reworked or easily repaired had been set. We would need Mason's skills to go further. I looked to the island. Both boats were still beached where the crew had left them. A pile of logs was stacked nearby and I could see several men sawing and planing them. I gathered the more capable men still aboard and told them what needed to be accomplished before Mason returned, then we shuttled half of the crew back to the *Panther* to start what work we could on her.

Halfway between the ships, with a unique vantage point to study both their riggings, I remembered my idea. Once aboard and after issuing orders, I went below to my cabin. There I took paper and pencil and started to sketch the rigging of the two schooners. The ships were slightly different, but with a bit of work, we could rig them the same. The *Panther* would be disguised and we would have duplicate parts for each ship. I started to draw and was so involved in my work that I jumped when I saw a man standing at the cabin door.

Not sure of his intentions, I covered my sketches and stepped back toward the shelves behind me that held the brace of pistols I had found hidden in the bunk of the pirate ship. I nodded. He entered and put his hands out, saying something in a strange dialect that sounded oddly French. I had been around Lafitte's crew and knew the singsong sound of Creole. This was close but not quite the same. I looked at him blankly, not understanding. When he repeated himself and continued to approach, I reached for one of the pistols. He yielded a few steps, backing into the passageway, but kept his gaze fixed on me. There we stood facing each other, both unable to communicate.

"He says he knows these gold bars and says there are many more," Shayla said bitterly just before she appeared in the doorway.

I kept one eye on the man while I watched her sidle past him and into the cabin. "You know his language?" I asked.

She shot me a withering look, one that only a woman can give, telling me without any words that I was a dullard.

"Seems I might be more valuable to you than you think," she said.

"They slighted you. I did what I could," I said, immediately regretting my tone.

"You dismissed me," she said and turned away.

"Can we put this aside for now? Let's see where this leads," I pleaded.

Shayla turned around. "It'll cost you some of that gold he's talking about."

I looked at the man and back to Shayla. "I'd split my share with you until I can get you voted in?"

Shayla shrugged, silently telling me we weren't finished, but for the moment, she had been placated.

I turned to the man at the door. He was a large man, and, though he appeared to be in the prime of his life, I noticed small signs of aging. The veins on his hands stood proud, and his ebony skin belied the wrinkles and splotches that normally show with age. I could see the small lines around his large eyes and the distinct crease that outlined his jaw. There was something different about the man, and I recalled the air of authority with which he'd carried himself with the other members of the crew. I could also tell he was getting fidgety. I lowered the pistol to set him at ease.

"Please ask him to explain," I prompted her.

They spoke for several minutes and I waited patiently for her to translate. I glanced back and forth between them as they talked, but I couldn't help but linger on her. Finally, the man grew silent and Shayla turned to me.

"This is Pierre," she said. "He has little English or would speak for himself. He was a man of some importance in Haiti during the slave revolt of 1794."

I remembered the revolt well. I had been a boy in Holland then, and it was all the talk about how the slaves had taken the island from the French. A decade later, the news was more disturbing. The liberated slaves had massacred almost the entire white population. This was unsettling news to the Dutch and

English who made fortunes from their holdings in the Caribbean. The ratio of slaves to whites on many of the islands was as much as ten to one and they feared more uprisings.

Though she recounted much of what I already knew, I listened carefully, trying to sort out the foreign-sounding names. It seemed that Pierre had been high in King Henri's cabinet until he had fallen out of favor for advocating for the people. She paused and turned to me.

"I'm sorry, but I cannot understand all the political nuance." Turning back to Pierre, she continued, "Henri must have feared him and sold him into slavery."

Tears welled in her eyes and I suspected there was something else, something more personal than the Haitian power struggle. "Is that all?" I asked, not failing to notice the sympathetic look they exchanged.

She turned away from him. "He says there was a deal with the English that many thought would beggar the island. They were to pay an enormous sum in gold, and England would ensure they were accepted into the community of nations."

I had heard about this as well but remembered that very little had been paid.

"Henri accumulated the gold, often stealing from his own people. He acted in good faith with a few small payments, but over the years he became paranoid and changed. He convinced himself that the French would take the country back, despite his alliance with England."

"But what of the gold?" I moved forward on my chair, anxious for him to continue. Pierre continued, speaking passionately to Shayla.

"He was in charge of the construction of the Citadel, a

massive fortress in the mountains. There were several large hidden vaults he was forced to construct for the treasure, but before it was completed he was taken and sold as a slave."

"Is there any indication of the size of the treasure?" I asked.

"That's a bit hard to interpret, but if governments were involved, it's probably large."

"Will he lead us to it?" I asked, focusing on the big man's face. By the tone of her voice, I could tell she was asking more questions.

"For his freedom and a portion of what you recover," she said.

"He's already free. What kind of split is he asking? And let him know I cannot make this decision alone. I have to sell it to the crew," I said.

They spoke for a minute. "Half," she said.

That was too much. Rhames and the men would never accept such a large share leaving their coffers. "Tell him we'll have to talk to the other men," I said, not relishing the task.

CHAPTER TEN

I sat on deck, deep in thought, avoiding the looks of the men as they went about their duties. Despite the prospect of treasure, I was morose. The flotsam and jetsam found on shore brought back memories of our pirate past. How many men had needlessly died over our greed? Rhames had found no sign of survivors. To that tally I now had to add the men from the frigate.

My concerns moved further afield. We had dropped a log line the night before and observed a two-knot current. It had been twenty-four hours since the attack. Simple math put the debris coming ashore on Grand Cayman sometime the next day. No doubt it would be found and recognized as being from the frigate. Our window for repairs had just shrunk.

It was late now and the moon had risen. Looking into the rigging, I was pleased to see how much work had been done. The freedmen were fast learners. It would only take a few days to fabricate and step the mast on the *Panther*. The pirate ship would be ready sooner. If Rhames agreed, he could use her to patrol the area for any sign of trouble until the *Panther* was seaworthy. I thought about taking the raft over to the pirate ship to discuss it with Rhames but decided against it. I didn't want to infect anyone else with my mood.

The man on watch was glad when I relieved him. I was restless and wouldn't sleep. My mind, still heavy with death, turned to the gold. I knew it would only take time and a strong argument to sway Rhames, but we were seafarers, and a trek into the mountains of Haiti was not in our favor. I sat on the bench by the helm. The weather portended by the morning sky had not arrived. Without the expected rain, I would need to check the fresh water stores. With this many men aboard, I knew we had to be low.

Taking a lantern, I climbed down into the hold. I did my best not to wake any of the sleeping men sprawled on the deck and thought about postponing my inspection when I heard whispers from the far corner. It wasn't idle conversation but a council of sorts. Five men were engaged in a heated discussion, their voices held low. I recognized Pierre's voice among them. He was speaking forcefully, but I was unable to understand what he said.

On a ship, secret meetings were bad business. Mutinies were planned in such ways. I thought of our conversation earlier and wondered if Pierre didn't mean to take one of our ships to Haiti and go after the treasure himself. I needed to get a handle on the situation and break up the group. Pretending to trip over a crate, I cleared my throat. The men fell silent. I wanted them to know I was there without alarming them, so I hummed as I moved past the barrels, checking them for water as I went, but I could still feel their eyes on me.

If there was a threat, this was not the time to deal with it. I nodded to the group and took my time checking two other barrels before making my way to the ladder and climbing back on deck. Relieved to be in the air and away from the intrigue, I sat back down and tried to recall anything I'd heard that might shed light onto the men's discussion.

"Why don't you go below and get some rest?"

I jumped when I saw Mason standing by the wheel.

"Can't solve the problems of the world by yourself," he said and lit his pipe.

I filled him in on the French captain's log and Pierre's claim on the treasure. At the mention of the gold, I saw the bowl of his pipe glow brighter. The story of the men below was another matter, and we agreed at first light we would question Pierre.

I left Mason at the helm, walked gingerly around several men sleeping on the deck and made my way below. The cabin door was closed and I took a breath before opening it. Mason was right, of course. Despite our earlier reconciliation, an ongoing domestic feud betrayed weakness to the crew. Those that hadn't witnessed Shayla jumping from the pirate ship during our meeting had surely heard about it.

The door opened silently and I stepped in. She was asleep on the bunk, the moonlight washing over her hair and highlighting the impish grin on her face. I couldn't wake her. Instead, I sat in the chair and just watched her.

"You could have made yourself a bit more comfortable."

When I heard her voice, I realized I had fallen asleep. Sunlight filtered through the stained glass windows, and Shayla sat on the bunk, pulling a comb through her hair.

"I didn't want to wake you," I mumbled.

"Dear me. A proper gentleman," she said, pulling her hair behind her head and tying it with a piece of cloth.

"You know I stood up for you," I stuttered, realizing I was placing myself under her judgment. "It just didn't go like I planned with the men."

"No, it didn't. But I'm a patient woman. And now with William dead, I expect I'm a bit more valuable."

It wasn't forgiveness, but the bitterness was gone. For the first time, I thought of how precarious her position was. She and her father were now without a home and at the whim of me and my crew.

Shayla motioned me over and I sheepishly moved to the bunk and sat beside her. "If we're together, we're together," she said. "That means the good and the bad."

I saw the trap, but I didn't care to avoid it.

***

Mason had the crew divided into three teams, with each assigned a specific duty. I had impressed on him the night before that we were not as safe as we thought, and from the looks of the men as they worked, the message had gotten through. I nodded to the work party and headed to the stern, where I climbed down to the raft and pulled myself across to the pirate ship. It was time to reach an agreement with Rhames.

I came onboard the pirate ship and found Rhames at the forepeak, pulling a line through a pulley to tension the forestay. He grunted acknowledgment, and not wanting to take him away from his work, I jumped in to help.

By lunchtime, the ship was ready for canvas and I looked across to the *Panther*. Mason was supervising the three crews as they shaped the fittings where the logs would be joined together to form a new mast. It was tedious work, I knew, and required the skill of a master carpenter. Even with Mason's expertise and the size of the workforce, the repairs to the *Panther* were two days behind those of the pirate ship.

I went to the open water cask on deck and drank from the ladle. Rhames joined me. "Slow going, eh?"

"We should have a word," I said.

He nodded and we went below to the captain's cabin. The room was much as I had left it, but I couldn't help but notice the collection of empty rum bottles had grown. Rhames had made it his own.

"You and the men still feeling the need to plunder?" I asked.

He rubbed the stubble on his face, a reminder of his past. "It's what we know."

"You saw what the Navy did to Gasparilla and the *Floridablanca*. England, France and Spain all have squads out looking for pirates. I'm afraid our vocation may be at an end."

He looked down at the deck. "I suppose you have a better plan."

I went to the door and opened it to make sure no one was eavesdropping, then came back inside. "I do. That gold bar in the chest."

"What of it?" he asked.

"What if I was to tell you that there is one hundred times that?"

I had his interest.

"Go on," he said.

I told him everything I knew about the treasure and about Pierre, including the conversation I saw him and his men having in the hold the night before.

His expression changed with that piece of information. "That seals it then. If that man is plotting, we need to put a stop to it."

"So we remain together as one crew?" I needed to hear him say the words.

"I'll put it to the men, but I expect that gold bar has their attention."

"So Haiti?"

"Haiti it is," he responded, and we grabbed each other's forearms, both infected with the lure of gold.

CHAPTER ELEVEN

The dawn was just breaking when we weighed anchor and set off together. I was anxious to be out of these waters. By my calculations the debris from the frigate would have washed up on the beach at Grand Cayman the day before, and if there was pursuit it would be here soon. It had taken the last two days to make the *Panther* seaworthy, but we would need more time to disguise her. While we completed the work, the pirate ship, renamed the *Caiman*, was out for sea trials. Rhames assignment was to scout the other island for survivors and patrol the area.

At first the trim of the *Caiman* was better and she moved ahead, but Mason took it as a competition, and after he was comfortable that the new mast was sound, he worked the crew relentlessly until we pulled even and then ahead.

I had to admit relief when the bluff fell below the horizon. As the hours ticked by I had become more anxious and constantly scanned the seas for any ship flying the Union Jack.

There had been no time to deal with Pierre and the other men. Our first order of business was to get underway, but now, as the boats cut easily through the light chop, tacking every few miles to hold the course just off the wind, it was time.

Rhames and I had met and agreed to a truce, or more of a contract. It was clear that he commanded the *Caiman* and treated it as his ship, but the bulk of the treasure remained with me on the *Panther*. The captured pirates had been enlisted as part of his crew and we had decided that until we knew the mettle of the men, the treasure would be safer with Mason and me.

Mason assigned the helm to one of the freemen who had an aptitude for navigation and we called for Pierre to come below to my cabin. The meeting had been staged in a way to make him comfortable. If indeed he knew of the treasure and where to find it, we would need his help. Of course, he would want something in return, but without him, the enterprise was dead.

We sat around the table and I offered him wine, which he accepted, smiling as he brought the glass to his lips and tasted the sweet Madeira. Shayla sat to the side and translated.

"You've every right to meet with any man on this ship, but if there is unrest I need to know about it," I started, trying to put him at ease with my tone, though I knew he didn't understand the words.

"I wouldn't say it's unrest, Captain. More like homesickness." He drained half his glass while she translated. "Some of us are not made for the sea, as you have probably observed. We miss our homeland. It was that we were talking about when you came across us. Merely how to talk you into taking us home."

If his intentions were truly this, then we had the foundation for an agreement. "What of the treasure? Would you seek it out?"

"Though I suspect where it is hidden, I do not know the current political climate in my country. It would be a surer enterprise with your men and ships," Shayla translated as he finished his wine, pushing the glass toward me to be filled before continuing.

"How so?" I asked, refilling it.

"The terrain is brutal. The mountains are high, some even covered with snow. The ravines are steep and treacherous. Then there are the bands of escaped slaves and natives who trust no one and would slit your throat before they asked your name."

"And what would you do if you found it?" I asked, trying to get to his motivation. Once I knew what drove him, it would be a simple matter to control him.

Shayla listened closely as he talked and started, "Our nation has no chance if we cannot trade. It is all dreams these leaders have to be self-sufficient and not have to rely on the outside world, but that is not the way things work. They are just trying to enrich themselves, leaving their countrymen in poverty. Without trade we will become impoverished and seek wealth from within instead of trading with other nations."

His acumen was sharp and from what I knew of the island and the effect of greed on men, he was correct. Unless they could start paying off the English and become a recognized nation, they would falter at every turn. "You would give the treasure to the English to satisfy the agreement?"

He looked at me and shook his head. "To those treacherous bastards, not a penny more than will keep them interested. They and the French are waging war across Europe. They need every ounce of gold they can find." He pushed his glass forward again.

"And what happens when we find the treasure?" I asked, ignoring his glass.

Haitian Gold

"I would think for your help we would split the treasure."

The stakeholders: Rhames, Mason, Red, Swift, Phillip and I had talked about a deal before we had sailed and all agreed that a quarter was fair. If the treasure was indeed what he claimed there would be enough for everyone. There was also no way that we could penetrate the interior of the island without his help. White men roaming around the Haitian mountains would be killed on sight. Finally, after several terse exchanges, he agreed.

"Right, then. We have a deal," I filled his glass and went to the sideboard for the French captain's chart of the island. I laid it on the table and all three of us rose and studied it.

"Where do we make port?" Mason asked.

Pierre placed a finger over a small cove and spoke to Shayla.

She paused before translating. "You'll want to stay to sea around the Isle de la Tortue, what we call Tortuga." I looked at Shayla to elaborate and she shrugged, then asked him another question.

"Pirates," she said.

I didn't like the look of the cove. It was protected, but too exposed. I told her my concerns and waited while they spoke.

"There is a river here. He says that once we are several miles inland there is no one that can contest our boats and weapons. The ships can wait here." He pointed to a large enclosed bay.

I didn't like the looks of that either. The estuary was large but the entrance was narrow and we could easily be blockaded inside. There were several Bahamian islands close by: Great Inagua and the Turks and Caicos to the north, where the ships could hole up while we made our journey into the interior.

I had to think quickly, so I took to the rigging. Shayla

followed behind me, but she must have sensed my mood and left me to think. We needed the strongest men on the expedition and Mason was the logical choice to command the ships in my absence. I decided on Rhames, Lucy, Blue, Red and myself from our crew and Pierre and four of the other natives to accompany us. Ten people would be small enough for two boats, but a large enough force if we needed to fight.

"I can tell from your mood that you've made a decision," Shayla said and moved closer.

I enjoyed being here with her and let the silence encompass us for a few minutes. We would have several days before we sighted Tortuga and I decided to put off telling her our plan. "We've got something to work with," I said elusively. Of course she didn't let me off that easily and questioned me until she had most of the story.

"You're going to leave me, then," she said.

I left the comment in the air when I saw Pott on deck for the first time in days. I went to kiss her, catching only her cheek when she turned her head away and climbed down.

"You're looking better every day," I said to the man and he smiled.

He nodded. "May I ask our destination? Jamaica is to the south."

I was surprised at his dead reckoning. We were heading east through the Windward Passage between Jamaica and Cuba. An idea came to me that would serve two purposes. "I was thinking about taking you ashore in the Bahamas. Great Inagua." There would be little in the way of force there, but it was a large enough colony to have a magistrate to take his testimony. We needed to provision for the expedition, and having to sneak into

Haiti, I didn't expect to find a trading post willing to deal with us there. If we had a good audience with the magistrate we might even leave one of the ships there while the other took us across to Haiti. I went to the helm to give the new course.

I called up to the rigging to fly the red pennant that would signal the *Caiman* to our side and waited. It took a half an hour for the two boats to come together and Rhames stood across from me. I told him in vague terms, as we were in easy earshot of the entire crew, that we were diverting to the Bahamas, where Pott would testify and we would provision the ships.

He had little choice other than to go along with us until we could speak privately, and he called to the helm of the *Caiman* to follow our course.

CHAPTER TWELVE

We turned to the north after passing the tip of Cuba and our sails greedily grabbed the trade winds blowing from the southeast. Having sailed these waters only weeks before, we had decided it was better to stay away from Jamaica. If the governor of the Caymans had sent warning to any other colonies, the news would have reached Kingston first. Staying off the coast of Spanish Cuba was a safer bet. In the distance we could see the mountains of Haiti off the starboard rail and Pierre joined me at the wheel.

Great Inagua was fifty miles off and with our current speed of six knots we would make her sometime late that night. Every chart I had seen showed a dangerous reef to the south, near the only town. Rather than chance the shoal in the dark, I decided to furl the topsails and reef the mains. The order was carried out efficiently and I immediately noticed our speed drop. The log line dropped and I waited for the call. We were down to three knots, putting us off the coast late the next morning.

Shayla saw Pierre by me and came over. I smiled at her. "Can you ask him if he's made a list of what we need?"

She listened while he spoke. "Yes, but he's not sure whether we can find the supplies."

We'd been improvising for so long, his nervousness didn't bother me, but looking at the mountains in the distance, I reconsidered. They rose high above the sea, their tops hidden by the low clouds.

I steered, enjoying the open water and good conditions. My mind was clear for the first time in weeks. Without the plague of Rory, our ship's hold full of treasure, and a new adventure on the horizon—life was indeed good.

We approached the harbor in Great Inagua the next morning and saw a half dozen ships anchored off the coast. With the glass in one hand I climbed into the rigging to evaluate the situation. Thankfully, they all looked to be traders. His Majesty's Navy was not represented. The harbor was deep and well protected. Both boats were soon anchored.

I called for Pott, and along with Mason and two crewmen we climbed down to the waiting skiff. The governor's man seemed nervous and I hoped he had not changed his attitude.

"You ready for this?" I asked him.

He nodded. "It may not be as easy as you think. I'm committed, but you have to know that each of these islands is a man's fiefdom and there's no telling how he will react."

I knew he was right after our dealings with the governor in Grand Cayman, so I left him to his thoughts. There was no future for him if he crossed us.

The men rowed the easy quarter mile to the town and I stood on shore for the first time since leaving Cuba weeks before. I swayed back and forth, waiting for my legs to adjust, as we walked towards the center of the small city.

The buildings were much the same as Grand Cayman: mud

daub huts with several more substantial structures near the center of town. We went to the first stone building and asked where we could find the governor's representative. A toothless man gave us a queer look and pointed down the street to a small rise where a wood-framed house stood, its windows wide open to the sea breeze.

I sent Mason and the men to look for provisions. Pott and I walked alone to the house. I knew what we looked like and did not want to alarm the man before we had a chance to explain ourselves. A servant met us at the door and left us waiting for the magistrate in the foyer, where we stood for almost half an hour without refreshment. Even the governor of the Caymans had been more hospitable. The arrival of two unknown ships had surely been brought to his attention and I worried about the delay. Finally the servant reappeared and led us to a balcony off the back of the house, where a middle-aged man sat, balding and wet with perspiration.

Without rising, he introduced himself in a gruff tone through a cloud of cigar smoke. "Thomas Milword, at your service."

I introduced myself and when I told him Pott's name, I caught a brief change in his expression. "We have two ships anchored in the harbor."

"What's your business here?" he said.

I saw him studying Pott without trying to be obvious and wondered if the two men knew each other. "Just a quick stopover to provision." I ventured a glance at Pott for confirmation, but he was staring at the floor.

"Don't have much but salt, but if you've money, we'll take it —and not ask too many questions." He laughed.

"There is one other matter we would like to broach with

you," I said.

He looked at Pott and I knew there was something between the men. "Mr. Pott would like to testify to the activities of our crew over the last few weeks."

"And why is that?" he asked, now openly staring at the man by my side. I felt him slither behind me.

"We had a bit of a problem in Grand Cayman. A misunderstanding with the governor there and we would like to get on record with a British authority what happened. Mr. Pott was in the governor's employ and can bear witness to everything that transpired."

"So, Pott. I thought it was you," he said.

Pott's expression remained stoic. "Yes, Thomas."

I tried to decide from their faces whether this was a good or bad development and quickly decided it was the latter. There was no love lost here.

"May we have a word?" I asked the magistrate.

He puffed his cigar and let the smoke clear before responding. "I think not. Guards!" he yelled.

I looked around, but there was no place to run. We were on a second-story balcony at least a dozen feet from the ground. Seconds later, two uniformed men emerged and Pott was taken into custody. I got up to protest but, realizing it was futile, I looked to see if there were more men waiting for me. Pott had been right about the power-seeking men running these islands. The magistrate and I stared at each other for a brief second.

"If you are innocent as you say, there will be no problem with a search of your ship."

There was nothing to be done now. A negative response would have Pott and me in adjoining cells. I nodded, turned and, with my heart beating so hard I could feel it in my ears, left the house.

I tried to slow my pace and appear unworried about what had happened. As I made my way down the path to the water, I looked back to see Pott being led inland.

I met up with Mason and the men at the skiff. I told him of the arrest and we were silent until the skiff reached the stern of the *Caiman*. This was where Rhames excelled and we needed to bring him up to date on the events. I called Swift and Red over and the six of us moved to the rail out of earshot of the crew.

"Leave the bugger," Rhames said after we told him what had happened. "There's nothing good going to come out of that needle-nosed, penny-pinching piece of lying crap," he spat.

I expected this from him and let him finish his tirade. "He's all that," I agreed. "But we need him. The magistrate has no love for him and will likely torture him to get him to say whatever he wants."

"We're already labeled pirates. What's to change that?" Red asked.

My plan to clear our names had failed and I saw its flaws. "Some of the silver in the bilge will," I said.

They stared at me, wondering why I hadn't learned my lesson about giving away our treasure. I had tried before to negotiate with William Bodden, the governor of the Caymans, for a Letter of Marque, but that too had failed. "Captured, Pott can do us more harm than good. I'm betting that if we bring a few of those silver ballasts to the magistrate and tell him it's the crown's share from the wreck, he'll change his tune. Maybe promise him a share of the treasure in Haiti for his protection. There's little chance for him to make any coin on this spit of sand. I've got a plan to make him a deal he can't refuse."

They fought me at first, but after explaining the alternative and having our ship searched, they finally agreed. It was one thing to use some of the silver ballast to gain favor, another to reveal Gasparilla's treasure.

***

I went alone to the magistrate's house, not wanting to endanger anyone else if my offer went badly. I knew there was the risk that he would imprison me and take our ships, but without any military force in the harbor, I expected he would negotiate.

It was near dark when I was led back to the balcony and I smelled the cigar smoke before I reached him. By his side on a small table was a half-empty bottle of rum.

"I'd offer you some, but I prefer to drink alone," he said.

I ignored the lack of hospitality and opened the burlap sack that I brought, carefully removing one of the ballasts.

"What have you brought? Nothing special there if you ask me." He drank from the bottle.

I had planned it this way, wanting a bit of drama to keep him interested. I also wanted to prove that we had recovered the treasure from the sea, something that he would need us alive for if we were to do it again. I took the dagger from my belt and struck the coral off the casting. He leaned forward and stared at the dull metal beneath the barnacles.

"Bloody hell, if it ain't silver," he said.

I had his attention now. "Recovered legally from a wreck in Cayman waters. We had a deal with the governor, but he got greedy and wanted it all. That is why we fled. Pott can attest to that."

"Pott can't attest to shit," he spat.

I wondered what their history was, but decided this was not the time to pursue it. "I'm here to bring you this as the crown's share." I pulled the other casting out and he smiled.

"Now, what have we got here? A pirate with integrity. That's a rare find. Maybe I will have a drink with you after all." He yelled for a servant, who brought a glass. The bottle was good enough for the magistrate.

He poured me three fingers and I sipped the amber liquid, almost choking at the harshness of it. He must have seen me because he laughed.

"Not the fine stuff you're used to, eh? This rock pile gets what it gets."

I had him now. "We are looking for a partner." He raised the bottle and drank. "For your protection and a Letter of Marque, we will share anything we find with you."

"Treasure hunters, are you now? It'd be all fine, except only the governor can give you the Letter." He paused. "Protection and provisions, though, that I can help you with."

I was wary of how far this offer could cover us. "The Letter or no deal."

"You bring back more of that, in something we can broker, if you know what I mean, and I'll get your Letter."

That was as good as it was going to get. We would have a safe port close to Haiti, provisions for the ships and, if things worked out, a Letter of Marque.

"What about Pott?" I asked.

"That dog is mine. Call it a surety." He laughed and drank

deeply, draining the bottle.

CHAPTER THIRTEEN

We replenished our stores and under a waxing moon set out for Haiti. Although the trip was only sixty miles, it was into the wind and would require multiple tacks, making navigation difficult. Fortunately the mountainous island was visible from far at sea. By leaving Great Inagua in the dead of night we expected to arrive off the coast in time to anchor before sunset the next day.

Mason and I talked as he steered. I watched the hourglass, calling the tack whenever it expired. By tracking the time and staying forty-five degrees to our course with each tack, we could stay close to a straight course. Of course the wind and current would alter our attempt at dead reckoning, but hopefully get us within sight of the river. Between maneuvers we worked out who should go ashore and what to do about the ship while we were gone. We had left the *Panther* in Great Inagua with Phillip in charge, not needing both ships. Under the watchful and greedy eyes of the magistrate, I expected her safe. The crew had orders to finish the changes to her sails and we had left several of the men skilled in carpentry to complete the repairs from the frigate's attack.

Now the decision needed to be made about who would make up the shore party. I would go, of course, along with Rhames, Swift, Red, Blue and Lucy. We had already traveled many miles together and knew how each would act if things went badly. Pierre had asked to take two men, making us eight. That was the limit the longboat could safely carry. Mason would stay with the ship and we had set up a system of signals from the Chinese flares I had found aboard the pirate ship. He would patrol off the coast and wait for us to set off the rockets.

Shayla came on deck, leaving an uncomfortable space between us.

"What are your plans, then?" she asked.

Mason made an excuse to check something forward and left us alone at the helm. "Tomorrow we should be off the coast. I'd like to land a shore party before dark and get on with it."

"You've not said two words to me since we left Inagua. If you don't want me around, just say the word. I'm not the kind to waste time," she said and inched further away.

I had been avoiding her, knowing she would ask if she was included in the shore party. "Your French will be helpful," I offered to judge her intentions. Rhames and I had fought about it. Lucy, we both knew, could take care of herself. I had no idea how well Shayla would do, but without her to translate we had little chance of success.

She turned to me. "You don't seem pleased about it."

"And I'm not. There's no telling what awaits us on that island. Surely you have heard the rumors about their voodoo. And ..."

She ignored my concerns and moved closer. "I'd very much like an adventure."

Mason returned and I offered to stand watch until dawn. He

gratefully accepted and went below, leaving Shayla and me together under a star-swept sky.

Around dawn the wind picked up. The helm pulled to the weather and I sent the men into the rigging to reef the sails. The ride, so pleasant only an hour before, had turned into a struggle to keep the ship on course. Mason must have sensed the change and took over the wheel.

"From the look of the sky, we've got a storm on the way," he said and called an order to the men.

The sun crept above the horizon, lighting the clouds a brilliant red, and I feared the worst. The sky was ominous and the wind had already started to prove the point. Before long the first drops of rain hit the deck and the storm came on in full, the raindrops so fat and hard that they reduced visibility to a few feet. With every wave a stream of water came aboard the ship, drenching us. I couldn't help but notice how cold the rain felt compared to the seawater and I began to shiver.

Mason looked to be enjoying himself, the muscles on his arms bulging and rainwater streaming from his hair and beard. Our course never wavered. I did the best I could to assist him with the traverse board and keep watch. It was one of the men in the rigging that first spotted land and I climbed up to see for myself. We were still a ways off, but the mountains, their tops covered with the low clouds from the storm, were visible and the shoreline became more defined as we crept closer. A breath at a time, the wind died down and the storm passed, leaving us becalmed. We drifted, praying for the sun to dry us out and take the chill from our bones.

The clouds stayed thick and did nothing for our moods. Wet and cold, we moved slowly toward the coast. I called for Pierre and Shayla.

"Can you tell where we are?" I asked.

"He says the clouds make it difficult to see the peaks."

I followed his gaze as he studied the land. Just as I was about to turn away I saw a mast on the horizon.

"Sail!" I called up to the men in the rigging and put the glass to my eye. "She's at least a frigate and flying Spanish colors."

Pierre held out his hand and I gave him the glass. He put it to his eye and watched the approaching ship for a long time, then scanned the shore to the west. I followed his gaze to the east and waited for Shayla to translate.

"We are too far to the east." she said.

Mason reacted before I could speak and spun the wheel hard to starboard. The last place we needed to be with this much treasure, a good portion looted from Spanish ships, was here, with the eastern half of the island in their control. I called the ship to battle stations and Rhames unlocked the weapons locker.

"Can we outrun them or will it be a fight?" he asked, the question directed more toward Mason than me.

Mason took a long time to answer. "Unless we can reach Haitian waters before she catches us, it'll be a fight." He paused. "Even then there's no guarantee she will stop. She's a man-o'-war by the look of her," he added.

"What can we do to get more speed?" I asked.

"She's on a broad reach and moving well." He turned the wheel to port and pointed the bow toward land. The men adjusted the sails and I could feel our speed increase. "That'll give us an edge, if we don't hit a reef or those hills don't steal the wind from us."

I saw his plan and knew it was the only way. We needed to

skirt the coast and hope the mountainous terrain didn't block the wind near shore. The land was coming up fast.

Pierre pointed to the west. "There is the border," he yelled. "To the right of the point."

We were headed to a small point jutting out from the mainland. Suddenly the water exploded behind us. A range shot had been fired from the Spanish ship and fell only a few hundred feet off our stern.

"You've got to get more out of her," I yelled to Mason and ran to the rigging.

"This is all we've got," he called back. "Better get the cannon sighted."

The sails were humming, taut with the wind. I released my hold on the rope ladder and went from gun to gun. Rhames was already working the elevation screws and there was no need for my help. I went back to the rigging and climbed to the top of the mainmast, hoping to find a way out.

Water splashed the deck as the next shot fell only fifty feet short. They would soon have us in range. I turned to the land and studied the coast. What looked like a river mouth was just a mile past the point. From my vantage point I could see no breaking water indicating a reef. I scurried down to the deck, sliding on the still-wet boards, but gained my feet and reached the helm.

The spot was almost invisible from this angle, and I pointed to the coast. "There is a river mouth or inlet there. If we can reach it, we can turn and protect ourselves."

Mason turned a few degrees and we pushed for the spot. The rounds were coming closer, but as yet we were not hit. We were stern to her bow and she fired her bow chasers, surely smaller guns than her port and starboard. We were too far away for our carronades to return fire. We needed the tactical advantage of the river mouth. I looked back and saw the man-o'-war adjust her course to follow us. The gap held and at least for the moment, she stopped firing.

"Go right for the eastern edge. We can jibe and fire from our starboard guns." I went to help Rhames site the guns for their maximum effective range. We could make out the details of the shore now, and I looked back at the Spanish ship. She had turned slightly and just as I was about to call out, she rocked violently and released a broadside. Their range was right on and several balls crashed through the deck. I ordered men to man the pumps and went forward. There was no point in dropping the lead. We were either going to make it or become cannon fodder.

Slowly we entered the inlet and I looked toward land, surprised to see a large bay open before us. Mason called the order to jibe and drop sail. The *Caiman* coasted to a stop in the center of the narrow pass. I gauged the approach of the man-o'-war. She was pointed right toward us, her guns ineffective at this angle. With the narrow profile she showed, it would take a well-placed shot to reach her, but this might be our only chance.

Rhames ran from gun to gun making final adjustments, then waited impatiently beside me for the Spanish ship to come into range.

"Fire!" he yelled.

The *Caiman* rocked from the recoil of the guns, and the smoke obscured our view. "Reload," I yelled.

Finally the smoke dissipated and we could see the ship now. Our broadside had been effective, taking several sails down, and the bowsprit was dragging in the water. Her crew would need to make repairs before they followed us.

"We're in Haitian waters now, but this is a bad place," Pierre said. "It is too easy to be bottled up in this bay. We need to head west toward the river. From there we can take the longboat to the palace."

CHAPTER FOURTEEN

The lights, visible first as a glow in the sky and upon arrival displaying the size of the palace, made me wonder at the folly of the mission. Pierre had said it was opulent and a testament to the evil regime of Henri, and now, sitting in the bush, I could see it truly was. Every approach was exposed and we were forced to wait until dark to enter. The native Haitian was a different man here: he stood tall and spoke with authority. I had come not only to trust him, but also to like him, though I couldn't help but notice the looks that he and Shayla exchanged —as if they had some secret between them.

Pierre had wanted to go alone, but I had forced the issue. Without him we had no chance at the treasure. Blue was with us for his tracking abilities. If something happened to Pierre, he could get us back. It was two days since we'd left the *Caiman* to Mason with orders to stand off the coast. The wind was favorable, allowing us to rig a lateen sail in the longboat. We had made good time traveling west along the coast and found the river that Pierre said led to the palace called Sans-Souci. Along with Blue, Rhames, Shayla and I had left the others several miles downriver and followed Pierre across the easy terrain until we were in sight of the palace.

After catching our breath, we left the cover of the road, staying in the shadows of a short wall about a hundred feet from the main structure.

We were about to cross to the gate when Blue came forward.

"I wait here, Mr. Nick," he said.

I nodded my ascent knowing his distaste for buildings. He would also guard our exit. Pierre led the rest of us toward the rear of the palace, arriving undetected at what appeared to be a service gate, where he called out in French. A few minutes later a rotund man with an apron appeared from the shadows.

Pierre engaged the man in conversation. I couldn't understand the words and looked at Shayla, but she was intent on listening. By the time it was over, the tone of the man changed. He opened the iron gate and allowed us entry to the kitchens. Pierre led us through the labyrinth of ovens, work areas and storage areas to a narrow hallway.

Carefully we followed the corridor until we reached a staircase.

"You must wait here," Pierre said.

Rhames and I looked at each other, not wanting to be left alone in the confines of the palace.

Pierre noticed our distress. "It is beyond that door that he keeps his women. It is here that the map is hidden. I must go alone."

"Hurry," I said and watched him fade into the shadows. A minute later I heard whispers and the rusty hinges of a door opening. Rhames and I waited in silence, peering into the shadows and listening for any sign of pursuit. Finally we heard the hinges creak again and we pushed ourselves flat against the wall.

Pierre emerged from the darkness and came toward us looking defeated. He whispered something to Shayla.

"Shit," Rhames cursed.

"What of the map?" I asked.

She spoke to him and he held out a rolled-up parchment. He spoke again. "It seems Henri is dead, and the new leader is one of his old generals: Jean-Jean," Shayla translated.

Pierre spat at the mention of the name and, with a sense of urgency, led the way back through the kitchens.

Rhames and I looked at each other, neither of us happy at the development, but we knew we had no choice. So far we had been lucky and only seen a few cooks. From everything Pierre had told us about Henri's reign, he was a brutal leader, taxing heavily and indenturing much of the population. From his reaction to the new leader's name, nothing had changed. The servants and slaves would not turn us in. An argument, though, might alert a guard.

Pierre led us away from the palace. His stature was different and he had become withdrawn. Shayla stayed close to him, the pair whispering back and forth in French, convincing me further that something was wrong. Once we were out of sight, we stopped to catch our breath. Before I could ask her what they had been talking about, a shot came from behind us and we heard a man call out orders. Despite the language barrier I knew we had been discovered.

An hour later we were back at the river. "Hurry, get the boat ready," I yelled ahead of us. The crew jumped up and in minutes had the longboat in the water. We pulled hard on the oars and with the current in our favor were soon several miles downstream, where we stopped.

"They will be on foot. We have lost them for now," Blue said and drank from the stream.

"Let's have a look at the map," I said. Rhames and Red moved beside me. Pierre unrolled the parchment and held it the moonlight. It was not a map at all, but a plan of a building. The outline and what looked like rooms were clearly shown. "What is this?" I asked.

Shayla again translated: "The Citadel. The gold is here." He pointed to the plan. "Henri was rumored to have built a secret chamber under the fortress where he hid the gold and then killed anyone that worked on it. He stole this from the builders and hid it with the women before he was arrested."

We climbed back into the longboat and were soon floating downriver again. Once in the main current, I checked behind for any pursuit. Satisfied we were alone, I turned to Shayla. "He says it is a fortress—then how do we get in?" I asked.

"I suspect it has something to do with that plan," Shayla said, and spoke to him.

He turned away, apparently not ready to reveal the fortresses secret. Or maybe he was just as tired of having to speak through Shayla as I was. I could feel Rhames tense in front of me, but it was too dark and awkward in the boat to look at the paper. The first rays of light were in the sky now and we followed the river back toward the coast, making twice the time we had the day before with the current in our favor. Near the coast we reached a fork, where Pierre had us turn upstream into the new tributary. This was a slower and wider section of the river and we pulled against the flow through the morning, taking turns at the oars.

Later in the day the river started to narrow and move faster. Just ahead were the first rapids Pierre had warned us of. "We must leave the boats here. The snow from the storm is melting and the river further inland will be impassable," he said and got out of the boat. On shore he unrolled the paper and crouched down in the sandy soil by the river. He motioned us over and, with a stick, he drew a rough map. I recognized several features on the coast as well as the river. He placed two small rocks inland.

"Sans-Souci." He pointed to a stone. "Citadel." He pointed to the other and drew a light line indicating a road out the back of the palace.

He spoke again and Shayla leaned in to hear his words. "He says the road leads into the hills, but it is heavily traveled. We will have to cross the hills here and go in from behind."

Still wary of the pursuit I went to the boat. "Whether they are on foot or not, we need to press on," I said and looked for a place to conceal the boat. I happened to look up at the mountains, and, for the first time since my childhood, I saw snow. The clear sky revealed white-capped peaks. Pierre and I were the only ones who knew what it was, and we covered the boat with the surrounding brush while the rest of the group stared in disbelief at the hills. "It looks nice from here, but once you're in it, it's not so friendly." Coils of rope and bolts of cloth lay in a pile by the boat. We had brought supplies, anticipating that we would be in mountainous terrain where the going would be difficult and the nights likely cold.

With several hours of daylight left, we ate dried turtle, then loaded up the rope and cloth and headed out single file through the brush. Pierre worked tirelessly ahead, clearing a trail with one of the cutlasses, but the brush fought back and he was only able to create a narrow path. The sharp branches and fine teeth of the low plants cut our skin, leaving small rivulets of blood that the mosquitos used to find us, and soon clouds of nasty bugs swarmed us.

It was almost dark when we started to gain altitude, leaving the brush and bugs behind us.

"He says we should camp here tonight. That these hills are riddled with ravines and with the snow it will be dangerous to travel at night," Shayla said.

Just as he spoke, Pierre collapsed on the ground. She went to his side with water and when he didn't drink, she put her hand to his head. She turned back to us with a scared look on her face.

"He has a fever."

Lucy went to him, her bag open by her side. She lifted his eyelids and peered in, scolding us to move back and let her work. "Is very bad," she muttered and pulled out several pouches. I had witnessed her expertise in healing several times. She had healed me when I thought I was dead after being clawed by the panther back in the Florida Everglades.

"What can we do?" I asked. Without Pierre, our expedition was over.

"We need fire."

CHAPTER FIFTEEN

Fire can be a tricky business in the tropics, and after a storm like we'd experienced the day before, everything was soaking wet. We had already climbed out of the littoral range, leaving the coconut palms with their highly flammable husks behind. We split up and picked through the deadfall, trying to find the driest material.

I was shocked when I returned. What had looked like a simple scrape on Pierre's calf had swollen and turned bright red. In fact, it looked similar to my leg after that panther had gotten me. Lucy's frantic movements obscured her skill as she combined herbs.

"We need fire," she scolded me. "Now, the evil moves fast."

Rhames had stockpiled the material and squatted over a pile of twigs and bark. He tried the tinder we had collected, but it was too wet. Giving up on the natural fire starter, he spread black powder over the kindling and moved to arm's length, where he struck the flint. With a whoosh, the material caught and burned brightly for several seconds before the powder burned off. He fanned the embers to a small flame and started adding larger branches. Minutes later the small fire turned into a roaring blaze.

While we waited for the water to boil, Lucy pulled me to the edge of the clearing. "Something bad is here," she said.

"I can see that." I thought she referred to the wound.

"No, Mr. Nick," she said in a whisper. "It is the voodoo."

The island was famous for its black magic, but I had never thought it real before. There was nothing I could say to calm her. "I know you can cure him," I tried to reassure her.

"I do what I can, but the magic, it is strong," she said and walked away. I set the boiling water by her supplies, then doused the fire, not wanting the smoke to give our location away.

"What's that she told you?" Rhames asked me.

I was about to answer when suddenly Pierre's body shook as if possessed. He grabbed his chest and screamed in pain. Whatever had a hold of him subsided and we huddled around his body. Beads of sweat covered him and he writhed in pain. Shayla was beside him, doing her best to soothe him.

"Quiet him," I told her and took the group to the side. There was no reason to hide what Lucy had said.

"He spoke of this man named Jean-Jean," I said over my shoulder so Shayla could hear. "He knows Pierre is here."

"What do you mean? The bastard general put a curse on him?" Rhames asked.

"Is true. It is the voodoo," Lucy said.

I could tell by the look on her face that she believed it. There had to be something I could do to convince her that it was merely a scrape from a poison plant that Pierre suffered from.

Lucy went back to Pierre and held the poultice on the wound, working it back and forth while humming under her breath. "I can do that," I said. "You need to go look for what it was that he suffers from. There is no voodoo."

She looked at me as if I were a fool. "Surely there is. I have seen it as a girl. Look at the wound. That is not from any plant or animal we passed."

I looked at the clean edges of the cut. In truth, it looked like a knife had done the work. The incision was a series of zigzags, all equal in length and depth.

I didn't want to concede to her, but we had to try all options and get moving. There were surely troops out looking for us. "If it is a curse, what can be done?"

"I have seen things as a child. The magic is not strong enough to kill him. Without some of his person—hair, skin or nail clippings—the curse will not be as effective. The old woman at my village, she would make dolls and baptize them to remove curses."

"What can we do?"

"Mr. Nick. Maybe the snow will purify the wound," Lucy said.

I thought for a minute, wondering how snow could help, but remembered something from my childhood in Amsterdam. My mother had used snow to stop the swelling when I had hurt my ankle. If nothing else, it would give the men something to do. "Right then. Let's get on with it."

I called to Blue. "Take Red and Swift and fetch some snow." The light covering I had seen on these hills earlier was melted now, but above us on some of the north-facing hills I could still see white patches.

This might or might not be voodoo, but it could serve the same purpose for Jean-Jean. He would suspect we were stationary and the fire might have shown our position. Rhames and I set a perimeter and stood guard while the women fashioned a doll.

"This is a strange business we're in," Rhames said as the circles we were patrolling converged. "Maybe we should get out of here while we can."

I had the same thought, but feared Jean-Jean would be reading our minds. "We have to assume that Jean–Jean is as paranoid as Pierre says, and will be guarding any coastline that a ship can approach. If we are to risk it, we might as well have the gold to show for it."

He nodded and we continued our patrol. An hour later, the men were back with several cloth bundles the size of cannonballs. Water dripped through the bundles, and I guessed they had been much larger before they had started their descent.

"We'll take it to Lucy," I said, assigning them to the perimeter to patrol while Blue and I grabbed the bundles and returned to the clearing. I was shocked to see Lucy straddling Pierre with a knife in her hand. With a deft cut, she freed a swath of his curly hair and moved down his body, chanting while she worked, to his hand. She sliced his fingernails and placed the cuttings in a small bowl. Shayla kneeled by his side, holding him still.

The doll was crudely fashioned of material cut from his shirt, stuffed with leaves and colored with soot from the fire. Lucy took the bowl and stuffed the clippings into a hole where the head would have been. If we were not in such a serious situation, I would have laughed.

"We are ready. If you are an unbeliever, you must leave," she said.

I knew this applied to me, but was curious when Shayla stayed. Before I left, I took one of the bundles of melting snow to Pierre and covered the wound with it. He moaned, showing he was still alive, but didn't move or react otherwise.

I walked away and soon heard chanting from behind me. A few minutes later Shayla appeared at my side.

"It is done," she said firmly.

"Can I go back now?" I asked her.

"Yes. The spell is broken. He is conscious," she said and led me back to Pierre.

He was leaning against a tree trunk, drinking some of the snow that the woman had melted into a cup. Our eyes met, but his were still far away. I looked down at his leg. Water pooled around the wound and on the ground from the melted snow but the wound was clearly healing. The swelling was virtually gone, and the cut had become white around the edges rather than the bright red it had been earlier.

"You're looking better for it," I said to him.

He moved his head and I could see his eyes were clearing now, the fever leaving fast. He spoke to Shayla. "He thanks you for your assistance and acknowledges a debt. He thinks he would have died without all of you."

I wasn't so sure of that. It was my opinion that the snow had cured the wound, not the baptism of the doll, but I held my tongue. Whatever worked was good with me so long as we could keep going.

"Are you fit to move?" I asked him.

Slowly he rose to his feet and put weight on the injured leg. He took a few slow steps and nodded. We still had several hours of light left and I intended to make the best of it. With Pierre leading, we started to move out. The terrain soon opened up and became steeper. It was slow going, moving up and down through the foothills, gaining altitude as we went.

We reached the peak of a large hill and stood amazed at the view. Behind us we could see the forest drop into a valley, where it turned into tropical bush, which quickly yielded to the ocean. To one side were steep mountains covered with snow and reaching into the clouds. I turned to the west and got my first glimpse of the Citadel.

It was still far away, and the hundreds of cannon that Pierre claimed guarded her approaches were invisible. Nestled into a high hill, the fortress looked impregnable.

"Those walls were built by a slave force of twenty thousand men over a decade," Pierre said. "The blood of many men are on those stones."

I took a tactical eye to the area. A road, winding like a snake, emerged from a battlement on the east side. I lost count of the switchbacks as they faded into the lowlands. It was the road we had avoided, leading from the back of Sans-Souci, and now I could see that Pierre had guided us well to stay away from it.

Sheer cliffs guarded the east- and west-facing approaches. The rear of the fortress faced south, built into the ridge that looked like the spine of a boar and extended into the mountains. It was there that we would attempt to breach the stone walls. I scanned the terrain we would have to cross and saw two other low ridges. As the crow flew, it was less than a few miles, but the route we had to take would be much longer and harder.

CHAPTER SIXTEEN

I was thankful for the heat from Shayla's body entwined with mine, but it was still barely enough to ward off the night chill. I had shivered alone under the light blankets we had fashioned from the cloth we had brought, until finally she joined me. We had chosen to do without fire; the clear night sky and the glow of the moon would have betrayed us if we had lit one. There was some conversation about traveling at night, but the terrain we needed to cross was difficult enough in daylight. In the dark it would be deadly.

Pierre shook us awake before dawn and we moved to the outskirts of the camp, where we relieved Red from his watch to let him get what sleep he could before we moved out. We sat on a small outcropping of rocks just covered in sunlight. Pierre removed the parchment and laid it out on one of the boulders, orienting it the way the fortress sat. From our position I could just make out its outline in the growing light.

He pointed out the main features on the plan and then we shifted our gaze to the newly completed fortress, its cut stones and plastered walls now fully illuminated. Rhames came toward us and Pierre called out the names of the batteries in French.

"The foundations were complete and they had just set the gun carriages when he was arrested. There were to be three hundred and sixty-five cannon covering every approach. He says Henri was paranoid the French would invade in force and this was to be the last bastion of defense."

"Bloody hell," Rhames said.

Pierre spoke again. "Twenty thousand of his people were forced to work on it and many died on the walls," Shayla said.

I wanted to refine our plan before the rest of the camp rose. "The Batterie Coidavid is impossible to approach without being seen." I referred to the sheer, pointed face of the Citadel. It looked like the bow of a ship and dropped hundreds of feet into an easily defensible clearing. The road from the castle wound in front of the point to the east where it disappeared into the Batterie Royale.

Pierre pointed at the approaches and spoke to Shayla. "It is the western batterie we must enter. The defenses are low here and there is no gate. The Batterie du Prince-Royal is the only entry we can approach without being seen, but the terrain is difficult; some say impassable," Pierre said and pointed to the mountainous terrain behind the Citadel. "We will have to cross these two ridges and make the climb to the tower. From there we will have to find the entrance."

"Find the entrance? You said it's impassable," I questioned him.

"He says there are secrets to the Citadel. Like the room where the treasure is kept, there are several secret exits. That is why we need this plan." He pointed to several notes written in French. Shayla bent over to read them. "Here is the vault. These marks note the entrance, and here are the passages."

Secret vaults and passages intrigued me, but looking at the terrain, I had to admit I had doubts we would reach them. "Are there trails?"

"He says they are well disguised. A network was formed when they started the construction," she said and rose.

It was time to move out and we roused the others. The sunlight had taken the chill from the air, and I expected the last hour of sleep the rest of the group had gotten was the best. We ate dried turtle and broke camp. Before we started out, Lucy came up to Pierre with the doll that she had made. It had a string on it and she placed it around his neck to ward off any future danger. Though I didn't believe in the magic, I would take any advantage I could get.

We set out in a single line behind Pierre and started climbing into the foothills. With the exception of the northern exposures, the snow had melted, making travel treacherous. Rivers of water sought the least restrictive path downhill and that was usually the trail. Finally, when we reached the first ridgeline, the sun and heat started to dry the ground and we made better time. The southern- and western-facing slopes were passable now, but the northern slopes were still wet and we often lost our footing in the slick mud, grasping for trees and branches to break our fall.

By nightfall we were just shy of the second and highest ridge. Pierre found a hidden clearing with a stream nearby out of sight of the Citadel's walls. We washed the caked-on mud from our clothes and soothed our tired and scraped bodies in the cool water, then relaxed on the boulders warmed from the afternoon sun. The temperature had climbed steadily since morning and I expected the cold front had passed and the night would be more comfortable.

We posted sentries and the women laid out what little food we had left. Water was not a problem here, but we had exhausted our supply of dried meat. Without fire, there was little use in hunting. Lucy and Shayla had gone into the brush and returned with a basket of greens and mushrooms, but they did little to ease the hunger pangs that had already started.

The night proved to be warm and I slept well, but when the camp rose and assembled the next morning, I could tell by the mood of the group that the lack of food was already taking its toll. Rhames and Red led the grumbling and I had overheard bits of conversation between them yesterday about the folly of our mission. Without food, their patience would be thin. With at least another day of hard travel, I wondered what condition we would be in when we finally reached the walls of the fortress.

My spirits rose when we crested the highest ridge early that morning and could see down into the country below. The footing was better with another day of sun and we moved quickly, arriving at the bottom of the last hill leading to the walls near dusk.

The light breeze brought the smell of baking bread over the walls and my mouth watered. Pierre had the plan out, but I didn't need to know we were near the kitchens.

He pointed and spoke. "Here is the passage. The code says forty-four blocks from the southeast corner and six blocks high," Shayla said.

I had no idea how that was going to get us into the Citadel. The stone blocks were huge and looked well placed. We waited until the twilight had evaporated to darkness, all the while undergoing the torture of roast meat grilling above us.

"Could use some of that," Rhames said, sniffing the air.

"Best to just get the business done with," I said. "It'll be shorter work down to the coast." I knew this wasn't going to be true if we were successful. I had no idea how we would carry the chests of gold down the mountains, especially if we were noticed and pursued. I watched him sharpen his knife and replace the flint in his pistol. We were ready. Blue took Lucy and Shayla to the side. He would lead them in search of food.

One at a time, we ran across the clearing to the shelter of the wall. Pierre had picked a spot near an inside corner of the battlement where it was almost impossible to be seen from above.

We were at the wall now and Pierre started counting stones. Each block was roughly two feet long and we were halfway down the wall when he stopped and counted six high. With the handle of his dagger he started to work at the stone but nothing happened. Each chip at the mortar echoed into the night, and I stared up at the walls for any sign that we were heard.

Finally the block moved and he called us to help lift the stone down. Immediately air shot out of the void and I knew we had found the passage. The stones around it moved easily and I could see the uncured mortar flake away when we moved them. Two more stones came free and we were able to squeeze through the opening.

The passage was narrow with a low ceiling that forced us to walk hunched over. It was dark. With our hands against the rough-cut walls, we moved deeper into the building. The air grew colder as we descended and I almost fell against Rhames when we hit a series of stone steps. We stopped and waited while Pierre struck his flint and lit a branch wrapped with cloth that he had brought with him. It ignited, but from its sputtering light, I could tell there was not much air in the shaft. In the dim light I could barely see Pierre running his hands along the wall at the bottom of the last step. It looked like a dead end.

He turned to me, confused, and shrugged.

I squeezed ahead of Rhames and felt the wall. With the tip of my dagger I explored the crevices between the stones. The mortar was hard and cured throughout, not at all like the passage in the exterior wall.

"Let me see the plan," I said and took the paper from Pierre.

The group backed up slightly to allow us some space to unfold the parchment. I oriented it to our present situation and stared at the lines, waiting for the answer to present itself. It didn't and I turned away and stepped down the last step to the wall. I tried another stone and my dagger caught on something hard and stuck. The blade dropped and I bent down to pick it up. Just as I was about to rise, I saw a sliver of light from the adjacent wall.

CHAPTER SEVENTEEN

I picked up the dagger and started to pry the block out. It was larger than the ones outside and I felt the blade start to bend, but before it broke, the stone began to slide. Rhames joined me on the ground and we worked together, using a back-and-forth motion to free the stone.

I smelled the smoke of a cheroot just as the block moved free and knew something was wrong. Suddenly the entire chamber shuddered and something crashed above us. It was dark now and I suspected that we had triggered a booby trap.

"Why don't you come in and join us?"

The French accented voice came from the next chamber. We looked at each other, not knowing what to do. The opening was barely large enough for one man to fit through and he would be helpless, having to enter by crawling on his belly.

"Jean-Jean," Pierre whispered and extended his hand to Rhames. "Pistol."

Without a better idea, I nodded to Rhames, who handed him his flintlock weapon and stepped aside. Pierre got on his hands and knees, trying to see through the opening.

"Come, my old friend. I see you there," the man said.

Pierre reached an arm in and cocked the pistol.

"Wait," I called to him. "Quiet." I could hear something from above.

"It's water," Rhames said.

Just as he said it a torrent of water entered the chamber. It didn't take me long to figure out from the accumulation already at my feet that despite the size of the opening we could easily drown.

"Hurry! Through the hole."

The water was getting deeper as I urged the men through the small opening. Pierre was first and with the gun extended in front of him, he entered the adjacent chamber. The water was well above the opening when Rhames disappeared, leaving me alone in the chamber. The level was almost to my head when I took a deep breath and dropped into the flooded chamber. My eyes were open, but it was so dark that I couldn't tell. With my hands fanned out in front of me, I searched for the opening. My breath was almost gone when I found it and pulled myself through, gasping for air as I stood. Blinking the water out of my eyes, I saw the other men were already on their feet with their hands in the air. Two men moved behind me and slid the stone back into place.

A tall skinny man with his hair groomed to cover his ears stood in front of us with his hands on his hips and a smile on his face. Surrounding him were half a dozen uniformed men with rifles trained on us.

Two of the men came behind us, collected our weapons and knocked us to our knees, where our hands were bound behind our backs.

The leader slapped Pierre across the face. "You arrogant

slave," the man said in French and then turned to us and repeated it in English. "You may have hid the plan, but it was I who put the workers to death after the chamber was completed —but not before they told me its secrets." He started pacing the room, his boots echoing off the stone walls with every step. He was about to turn away, but faced Pierre again. "So this is how you did it." He pulled the doll from his neck and stuffed it in his pocket.

I wondered how the women and Blue had fared above, hoping the general had focused all his resources on us. Slowly, I looked around the chamber, lit by several oil lamps. It was empty. Whatever treasure had once been here was no longer. The stone walls were damp from the moisture of the soil around them and there was one steel door barring the entry. From all indications, the room had never been used.

"It is a shame, my old friend," the general started. "Your life has been wasted. First as a dog to the king, then a slave, and now you stand before me, clearly not knowing where the gold is hidden. That was the only reason I have kept you alive this long." He barked a command to the men, who followed him out of the room.

The door slammed and seconds later the lock turned. We were trapped in the room and I searched for anything that might cut our ties. "There is nothing of use in here," I said. It sounded like the water had stopped and Rhames helped me claw the stone from the opening. Water poured in, but quickly drained through a slot in the floor. I crawled back through the opening into the wet passage. Our torch was soaked and of no use. The corridor was pitch black, forcing me to climb the stairs hands first. At least the water had stopped, making it possible to reach the entrance.

Water still dripped from the ceiling but it appeared that the reservoir it came from had emptied. I turned my back to the opening to use my hands and was surprised when they brushed against steel. I moved them from side to side and up and down, but found nothing but the rough metal that wasn't there when we entered.

In my head I saw the device, realizing that once the loose stone was removed, the steel plate, which had helped contain the water, dropped, sealing the entrance and releasing the water. If we were to escape it would have to be through the Citadel. Defeated, I climbed back down and slid into the chamber, where I sat against the damp wall.

***

Several hours later we were awakened by a sound. The room was black. So dark that I couldn't tell if my eyes were open or closed. My legs were stiff and I had to use the cracks in the block to inch my way up the wall. Just as I reached my feet, the door banged open and I could hear men entering the chamber. The light was blinding and it took a minute for my eyes to adjust before I saw the tall man standing in front of me.

"You are the captain of ships?" he asked in English.

He was looking right at me. I wondered where he had gotten the information and was about to deny it when Shayla was pushed into the room and thrown to the floor. My stomach sank when I saw her condition: her clothes torn and face bloody. I knew in that moment that I would do anything for her safety and somehow get revenge for what he had done to her.

Pierre stepped forward to confront the man, but with a practiced move, he drew his pistol and held it to Shayla's head. My heart tightened in my chest and I tensed as if to move forward. Rhames sensed my anxiety and brushed against me, whispering that this was not the time.

"The woman tells me that you have some apparatus to dive underwater as well," he said.

"Yes," I said. If nothing else I needed to soothe him enough for him to lower the weapon.

"Very well, then. You have saved your lives—at least for now." He left the room, the men following behind him, the last one slamming the door.

I screamed for them to send food and water, but the door had already closed. I looked over at Shayla. "Are you all right? I swear I'll get revenge on that bastard."

She crawled to me and I dropped to the floor, letting her head rest on my shoulder. She placed her arms around me and I pulled her close, oblivious to our condition until Rhames broke the silence.

"Her hands?"

I looked up but did not understand.

"You lovestruck fool. They are not tied. Now save that for later and let's figure a way out of this mess," he said.

I pulled away and looked at her. We had just caught our first break.

"Untie us," I asked her. She fought with the knots in the dark, apologizing when she had to dig her nails deep into my wrists before the tie came loose. I shook out my hands and wanted nothing more than to hug her, but we had more pressing matters. Several minutes later we had the others free.

"I'm sorry. We got caught in the kitchens and they took us to the general. I didn't want to tell him anything." She started weeping.

I hugged her now and quietly reassured her that she had done nothing wrong. When I could feel her breathing even out, I asked again about Lucy and Blue.

"We split up in the kitchens. As far as I know they were not captured."

That did not surprise me and it gave me a glimmer of hope. Blue would know Shayla had been caught and would have followed. As if on cue, I heard scratching at the door and silenced the group. I put my ear against the steel and jumped back when the door vibrated, followed by a muted explosion. The door opened and Blue stood in the clearing smoke, waving us on. "Hurry, they must have heard the boom."

I was last from the room, looking back in the dull light to make sure everyone was out, and followed them up the narrow stairwell. At the top, Blue raised his hand to halt the group and we listened over our beating hearts for any sign of pursuit. He decided we were in the clear and he slowly opened the door and signaled us it was safe to proceed with a finger to his lips.

We emerged in a dark passage and moved toward a sharp bend. Blue went around first and waved us on. I had no idea where we were in the fortress, but my mouth watered when I again smelled food. Another turn and we entered the kitchen. There were several people working, but from the low light and lack of activity I assumed it was deep into the night now. A basket of bread caught my eye and I reached for it, handing a loaf to everyone. We stayed low, moving through the kitchen, passing through unnoticed and entered another corridor with huge storerooms on either side, eating the loaves as we went. Pierre had told me the history of the building. Henri, in his paranoia, had built in provisions for enough water and food to be stored to last five thousand people a year, and looking into the cavernous rooms, I could believe it.

Finally we reached a gate and I could smell the night air. Rhames went first and whispered back that it was locked. I shook the lock in frustration and was about to ask Pierre if there was another way out. My first thought was that they locked the gates during the night, which might have been accurate, except in this case it was a trap.

CHAPTER EIGHTEEN

The echoes of the rifles and ricochets of bullets off the stone walls of the corridor made it hard to judge the force against us, but I knew there was no way out except for the gate. Smoke from the guns obscured us. I thought we were safe until I heard an order in French and the firing stopped. My ears rung from the noise, but I could still hear the sounds of boots coming toward us. The smoke still hung in the air, acting as a shield. I didn't expect them to attack until they could see us.

Rhames hurled himself against the steel gate to no avail and we waited in silence for the men to approach. "Is there no other way?" I asked Pierre but got no reply. The smoke was just a haze now and we had only seconds. With nothing to lose I ran my hand around the stone joints surrounding the door. It was a habit of Gasparilla to secrete a key near any locked door as he was forever misplacing his. I thought the attempt futile and prepared for the worst when my finger hit something. The sound of metal on stone echoed through the quiet corridor when the key hit the floor.

Rhames and I bumped heads in our rush to retrieve it. It landed in my hand and I reached up for the lock. The key missed on my first try, but on my second, just as I heard the order to fire, it slid into the lock. I turned key, pushing the door at the same time, and we landed in a pile, with bullets flying over our heads. Pierre took the lead and Rhames the rear as we ran down the road. I grabbed Shayla's hand. "Run!"

Shots fired again. We ran on, but with each volley, I could tell they were getting closer. We were starting to slow and I was out of breath. With my last burst, I released Shayla's hand and ran to the front, where I caught up with Pierre and motioned him off the road.

"Our only chance is to lose them in the brush," I said.

He nodded and veered to the left just as another round of shots hit the rocks right behind us. We were in the brush now. I waited for Shayla and Lucy, who trailed about ten yards back, and pushed the women in front of me, urging them on. Blue was last and I asked him to cover our rear.

I was looking behind me instead of in front, worried about the pursuit, when I failed to see the group had stopped and I ran into Rhames. We both fell and I felt his hand around my mouth. Huddled together in the scrub by a large tree, we waited for the men to pass. They would quickly figure out we had left the road, but those precious minutes could buy our freedom.

Blue appeared at our rear. "Last man go," he whispered.

Slowly we started down the slope of the hill. We worked as quietly as possible, collecting scrapes and bruises as we stumbled on unseen roots and rocks. I was starting to get a good feeling about things when a bullet hit the tree by my head.

"They've found us!" I yelled the obvious. Speed was more important than stealth now. We started to run, hearing voices behind us. Every few seconds a shot could be heard, but the branches obscured us, giving them nothing to aim at. Suddenly the group stopped as one and we found ourselves on the edge of a rock outcropping.

The ravine was spread before us in the moonlight and I scanned the area for any escape. We were on a tongue of rock, projecting several feet from the cliff behind us and totally exposed. "Down," I whispered. The best we could do was to lower our profiles and hopefully blend into the rock.

An order was barked, breaking the momentary silence, and I clearly heard the simultaneous sound of muskets cocking. The sky lit behind us when the flints struck the primer pans and lead hit all around us. Red called out beside me and I looked over at him. Blood streamed from his arm where a bullet had caught him. Fortunately he was the only one injured.

With only seconds before they reloaded and fired again, I slid back toward our attackers, looking for a way out. Crawling on my belly, I pulled myself off the outcropping and back onto the dirt at the top of the cliff. I looked over the edge but found it too high to jump. I slid further to the left and just ahead I saw the tip of the rock and what looked like a dirt chute just past it. I whispered back to the group to follow my lead.

"Come on!" I called over my shoulder. There was no need for subterfuge now. I reached the chute and peered down the path, which looked like it had been carved out by the runoff from the storm. It gleamed in the low light, still wet from the melting snow following its course. One by one the group reached me. Shots fired again, but they were sporadic. We were flat on the ground and they hadn't located us yet.

"Go." I tapped Rhames on the shoulder. "We'll be right behind you." More shots fired, this time closer to our position.

"Bloody right you will," he said, crossing his arms over his chest and placing his feet into the slick mud.

I feared they would have their aim by the next round and pushed him forward, calling for Red and Swift to go next. The three men slid off the cliff. The women went next and then Blue. I took one last look behind me and saw the primer pans flash before pushing myself off.

My stomach dropped immediately and I felt like I was falling through the air until I hit the first bush. One of the branches caught my arm and spun me around. I was sliding backwards now and could see the men leaning over the edge of the cliff above me. They fired down, but we were already out of range.

I spun again after striking something hard and lost the feeling in one leg. The rock had slowed me enough to get my bearings and I sought out the rest of the group. Ahead of me I could see them all several feet apart, still sliding down the steep slope. I was able to use my feet to steer and soon found myself at the bottom of the ravine.

We stood slowly, each of us checking for wounds. Lucy was already by Red, wrapping a strip of fabric she had torn from her muddy skirt around his arm.

"You all right?" I asked him. He nodded and I looked at Lucy, who didn't seem as sure. There was no time to treat him further. I turned to Shayla. "Ask him if there is a river in this ravine."

"He says the headwater for the river to the coast is in the next ravine," Shayla said. "But there is one down there that flows by the capital. It is very busy and might be more dangerous."

I looked at the ravine below and the ridge beyond and knew that, even if we had lost the guards, there was no way we would make it over the imposing ridge in front of us. In our condition we needed the aid of a boat and the river.

I caught Rhames's eye and knew he agreed. Our best chance for survival was to find the closest water and steal the first boat we could find, dealing with the consequences later. "Does he know the way?"

"Yes, but he says they will be waiting. It is only five miles to the palace by road and another two to the coast."

"Right then," I said and stood. "Let's move."

Pierre led us through the drainage. The footing was better on the game trail he found, but every so often I heard a cry as someone stumbled or fell. I had Shayla beside me, my arm around her, trying to shepherd her safely through the tangle of vegetation.

We were close to the bottom by late morning and I could hear the sound of water running. With the sun had come the heat, and my mud-soaked clothes dried stiff and heavy, making it hard to move. At last we reached the river, if you could call it that. This far inland it was more like a stream, but we all fell to our knees and drank. After drinking our fill we washed the mud from our bodies and clothes.

There was a clear trail now and I saw smoke ahead. With any luck we could find canoes. I started down the path, but Pierre grabbed my shoulder.

"He says we need to be careful. The tribes this far inland are dangerous," Shayla said. "Henri took many of them as slaves over the years. They are wary of strangers."

I called Blue over and asked him to scout ahead. If there was trouble, he would sniff it out.

"Is bad here," he said and looked over to Lucy, who came by his side.

Haitian Gold

They disappeared into the brush beside the road and I waited a few minutes to allow them enough of a lead. We were just about to head out when I felt something prick my shoulder. Just as I looked down to see what it was, I saw Rhames and Red fall to the ground.

CHAPTER NINETEEN

The hut was dark and smelled of blood and feces. My shoulder burned and I remembered being struck by something. After that, I wasn't sure what had happened. When I tried to sit up, a wave of nausea overtook me, and I collapsed back onto the dirt floor.

A voice said something in French and I felt a blow to my groin. Slowly I opened my burning eyes and saw a figure above me that sent chills down my spine. He was dressed in tribal garb, with the fangs from a boar stuck through his ears and nose. White streaks outlined the grotesque features of his face and blood coated his arms. He said something and wound up to kick me again. This time I reacted and moved before the blow struck. He laughed—a harsh sound I will never forget.

I looked around the dark hut and saw the others scattered on the floor, still unconscious. I wasn't sure why he had started with me, but I would gladly take his punishment if it spared Shayla. Just as I thought it, he left me and started to move around the room, leaning down and inspecting the rest of the group. When he reached Shayla I crawled to my knees and grunted, trying to distract him.

He came back to me. I struggled to my feet and played the only card I had. "Jean-Jean mal." I spat in the dirt, guessing the evil man had to be hated by the natives.

His face aligned with mine and, when he moved close, I could see every pore of his skin. We were nose to nose and he let out another laugh. This time, though, it was not at my expense and he patted me on the back. A stream of guttural French came from his mouth, but I understood none of it and shrugged my shoulders. On his haunches, he slapped the ground in frustration. I sensed that I was on the edge of losing him and looked over for Pierre. He was not here. Shayla understood French, but I didn't want to endanger her, but then, after looking around the squalid hut, I realized it was not going to get much worse.

I pointed to her and moved my mouth, trying to tell him that she could speak his language. He nodded, giving me permission to go to her. She woke at my touch, but I could tell whatever had struck us was still in her system.

"Nick," she said.

I put my finger to her lips and moved my eyes toward the figure squatting in front of us. She gasped.

"What happened?" she asked.

"I told him that Jean-Jean was a bad man and he seems all right now, but I need you to translate." I could tell he was getting uneasy and I didn't want to go into much more detail in a language he did not understand. I sat beside her and we started a stilted conversation.

"He says he is the chief, but I can't make out his name," Shayla relayed to me.

"Where are Pierre, Blue and Lucy?" I asked.

"The others are separated. Pierre is not his enemy, but... it's really hard to understand his dialect."

I gave her a reassuring look.

"He says Pierre is in the clutches of evil." She turned to me. "If they are not enemies, then something else is going on here."

"What about Blue and Lucy?" I asked, turning to face him. He rose from the squat he had been resting in and stomped his feet. I looked at Shayla.

"He says the little people have powerful magic. I think he's scared of them."

"Can we see them?" I turned to him and pointed at my eyes.

Without a word, he left the hut, but looked back to see if we were following. I took the cue, got up and helped Shayla to her feet. She was a little uneasy, but gained her balance after a few steps. The clearing was deep in shadows, the daylight filtered by thick foliage above. The women were tending to their chores, but I could see them sneaking looks at us; the children were not so shy and started to follow until the chief scared them off.

He led us through the village, past the cooking fire, where my mouth started to salivate and I remembered how long it had been since my last meal. Near the river stood a hut, smaller than the others and set off to the side by itself. Two men guarded the entrance, but yielded to their leader. They averted their eyes as we ducked into the opening.

Pierre was strung up on a wooden rack, his arms and legs splayed and secured to the frame. "He looks like a prisoner to me," I said. Shayla went to the inert figure, then turned to the man and fired off a series of questions while I went to Pierre.

His face was covered with sweat and although his eyes were open I got the feeling he didn't recognize us. Shayla held his hand and suddenly his body tensed. A grimace like I had never seen before came over his face and he started to struggle against the restraints. I watched him, unable to understand or help, when his stomach seemed to knot up, the muscles tensed and stood proud of his lean frame. The convulsion lasted for another minute and then his body relaxed.

"Ask him what is happening." I turned to the chief, wondering what he had done to cause this. He surprised me with a look of concern bordering on dread, as if this was something out of his control. Shayla went to him and they talked quietly for a few minutes.

I stood by Pierre, wiping his brow with a wet cloth that I had found in a bucket by the frame.

"He is scared of the magic," Shayla said, coming towards us. "He says that Jean-Jean has a hold on Pierre and there is nothing he can do. He plans to sacrifice him to rid the village of the evil."

She started in again with the chief, the tension in her voice clear—she was pleading for his life. The chief turned away, but she grabbed his hands and her tone changed. Now it seemed that she was begging him.

I still wasn't convinced of the magic, but couldn't discount what I had just seen. "Tell him that Blue and Lucy have magic and they cured him before." Shayla turned back to him and translated. He became agitated and started pacing the room like he had a life-or-death decision to make. Finally he said something and left the hut.

"He says to stay here. He will fetch the pigmies," she said and came by my side. She placed a hand on Pierre's forehead and jumped back. "He is ice cold, but sweating."

We waited for the chief to return. In the meantime we could do nothing but comfort Pierre and hope that he didn't suffer another attack. The chief entered the hut a few minutes later with Lucy and Blue. I looked at them and saw the same cloudiness I had seen in Shayla's eyes. Both had their wrists bound behind them. They nodded to me and went to Pierre.

"She needs to use her hands," I said to Shayla. "Can you convince him?"

She talked to the chief, but before she could finish I heard Lucy start chanting something in a tongue I didn't understand. Blue joined in the chant and the chief moved next to him and together they stared at Pierre. I looked at Shayla, but she just shrugged her shoulders.

Together they chanted. Shayla and I stood back and watched. Finally Blue turned to me.

"The curse is back. Jean-Jean took the doll. He is doing this," he said.

I looked at Shayla, who turned to the chief and told him the story of the mysterious leg wound that had plagued Pierre earlier and how he had been cured. He stared in awe at Lucy and reached behind his back and pulled out a dagger. I started to move to stop him, but Shayla grabbed my arm.

"Wait," she whispered. "I don't think he means him harm."

She was right, and he cut the rope binding their wrists. He turned to us and started to speak. I could tell from his tone that this was serious and waited for him to finish and Shayla to translate.

"He worries for his tribe and believes we are his friends, but he is scared of Jean-Jean and the magic. If the evil general knows where Pierre is, he will attack the village."

Without warning he called the two guards into the room. They grabbed Shayla.

"Let her go!" I screamed and made a move toward the chief. He started talking again, speaking directly to her.

"He says that you must go and find Jean-Jean and bring the doll back or his village will be destroyed by the magic. He is holding me hostage to ensure your success."

I looked at the pleading look on her face and knew there was nothing I could do but go back and find the general. Not only was Pierre the only clue left to the treasure, but now my woman was in jeopardy.

"I will do it. Tell him."

She translated. He seemed to relax and ordered the men to let her go. She moved to me and I reached for her, but one of the men pulled her back. The chief began to speak again.

"He says that he will hold me and Lucy. We will be his guests and not mistreated as long as you accomplish your mission."

I looked at Blue and he nodded his support. Now I would need to rally the other men, and with no immediate reward for their efforts, a task I might not be able to accomplish. "Tell him to let Lucy help Pierre." At least she would be able to comfort him.

The chief ordered one of the guards to stay with her and we left the hut, the other guard staying close to Shayla. "Tell him we need food and supplies." I rattled off a list of things I thought we might need.

He nodded and I looked at her, trying to memorize her features, hoping this would not be the last time I saw her. "I'll be back for you—no matter what," I said.

"The woman. Pierre told me about his wife being held there.

Find her and she will help you. Her name is Cloe."

We gave a last look at each other, speaking our love through our eyes. I turned away and we went to the hut where I had first found myself. I woke the other men and told them of our predicament.

"What of the treasure?" Red asked.

"Forget the bloody treasure," Rhames said.

"He has Shayla," I pleaded.

"And now the bloody woman. I say we take one of their canoes and escape before they cook us alive. I've heard the stories."

"This is their land. They'll catch us," I said. He paused to think and I pressed on. I needed their support and hoped what I told him was not a lie. "Pierre knows where the treasure was taken. But without our curing him, he cannot tell us."

If there was one thing that could change a pirate's mind it was the mention of treasure. Their demeanor changed and we went to the cooking fire, where a meal had been prepared. The food was odd, but my stomach welcomed it. Just before we finished I saw several of the men turn to the brush and heard the sound of rifle fire. One of the natives fell and we threw ourselves on the ground, waiting as the bullets flew over our heads. Another man screamed. I tried to count the shots to get an idea of the force we faced, but only reached six before they stopped. Even if they were only a handful, with their firepower they could easily take the village.

Bodies slid silently past me and I saw one of the men with a blow tube similar to what Blue and Lucy used. I counted a dozen men move through the dirt and enter the bush, but lost them there. This was their territory and I could only hope they would prevail.

Shots fired again and I was able to confirm my count. It was a small squad that had found us, but I feared the gunfire might attract the other troops, who were likely nearby. It was quiet while they reloaded, but the silence lasted far longer than I expected. A random shot fired, followed by a muffled grunt. Suddenly the village men returned, carrying the rifles of the attackers. Rhames looked over at me and smiled. At least we had arms now.

CHAPTER TWENTY

It had taken all day to traverse the ridgeline separating the village from the fortress and now the Citadel walls were in the shadows cast by the setting sun. After a hard goodbye we left Lucy and Shayla to care for Pierre. Red had stayed as well. His wound from the gunshot had not been serious, but he did not have full use of his arm yet. Despite having one less man in our group, it gave me some security that he was with the women. Leaving Shayla was hard and I still remember the look on her face when I turned around for one last glance before entering the bush.

We had declined the offer of a local guide, preferring to keep our band together. Rhames, Swift, Blue and I had been through enough action to know each other's tendencies, and we had the trust only gained through experience.

Twice on our approach we had encountered Jean-Jean's squads out looking for us, but with Blue's skills as a tracker and bushman we had avoided them. Both instances had cost us precious time: our choices were to either hunker down and wait them out or choose a circuitous route to avoid them.

Rhames, Swift and I sat behind a rock outcropping that

screened us from the watchful eyes of the sentries we suspected were high on the walls of the fortress. We waited for Blue, who scouted ahead. I doubted getting close to the Citadel would be a problem now—this would be the last place that Jean-Jean would think to look for us. I worried about another squad coming across the village, but the tribe was alert now and we had seen firsthand that they were capable of fighting this enemy.

"Bloody crap being back here," Rhames said. "Thought by now we'd have a load of gold and be sitting on the beach waiting for the *Caiman* to pick us up."

"When was the last time anything was ever that easy?" I asked and both men laughed. Our mood was surprisingly light. We chewed dried meat and waited for Blue to return.

Just after dark he entered our small camp. "The evil man is not here," he said. "They say he has gone down the hill to the castle."

This was not good news. Sans-Souci, though only five miles down an easy road and not nearly the fortress the Citadel was, would be harder to enter. The vast majority of men from the fort were out searching for us, leaving access easier here. With their leader present, the palace would be at full force and, from the paranoia I had seen on the face of the twisted general, I suspected they would be on full alert.

We moved out right away, wanting to reach the palace before midnight, allowing us several hours of darkness to find the doll and escape. I wondered what afflicted Pierre, still not believing in the voodoo. It had been easier with the first injury, as I had known that the snow would reduce the swelling. I also suspected that the tea Lucy had made from the bark of a tree had something to do with it as well. This time I had no idea what to do. I had never seen a man in his condition.

We stayed on the road with Blue out front and Rhames as our rear guard, careful to avoid any contact. The road was empty and the going fast. The glow from the lanterns and torches of the palace was visible before the stone walls came into sight.

I waited for Rhames. "We should get off the road here and send Blue ahead," I whispered to him.

"Aye. With this much light we'll be standing out like a whore in church. The bugger'll find a way in," he answered.

We gathered in a small clearing off the trail and I explained my plan. I wanted to enter through the same gate Pierre had the other night and make our way to the women's quarters. Shayla had told me they were being held against their will, and I suspected they would help us. With any luck we might find the woman Shayla had spoken of before we set out. They would know how to reach his bedchamber and likely be our best source of help. Without them we would have to fight our way in and, with only four of us, the odds of even reaching the general were stacked against us.

Blue returned and we followed a small game trail that ran parallel to the road. I had the vaguest of plans that would rely heavily on luck, as most of our ventures did. Blue and Swift backtracked to a spot on the road out of sight of the gate and crossed to the other side. A few minutes later, a pebble landed nearby, the signal that they were in position.

Stealth was our aim, but we had no idea how many men we would have to get past, so we had our rifles primed and loaded. Ready just in case.

"Go," I whispered to Rhames. We crept closer to the edge of the path and I tossed a rock at the gate. Nothing happened. The next throw struck the steel, sending a loud clang into the night. We waited again and I wondered if the guard was asleep. Just as I was about to throw an even larger stone, I heard the sound of boots coming toward us and someone calling out in French.

The dart landed silently and the man fell to the ground. Blue's aim as usual was right on. A few minutes later, someone called out what sounded like a name from inside the gate and then we heard footsteps when no one responded. This man suffered the same fate as the other guard, and then we waited. I suspected the guards worked in pairs, and after the silence extended for several minutes, I moved to the wall adjacent to the gate and slid towards the lock with my back against the stone.

When the lock was within arm's reach, I peered into the corridor. The light from a lantern danced against the walls, allowing just enough light for me to see the keyhole. I bent down, pulled one of the men toward the gate and reached for the key ring on his belt. The third key worked.

"It's open," I whispered to the men and pulled the gate open just enough for us to slide inside. Rhames took the lantern and we moved down the corridor. The sound of men snoring came from the dark interiors of several half-open doors as we silently crept down the hallway. A hundred feet in, we reached an intersection and had to make a decision.

I had seen several illuminated windows on the right side when we approached and guessed these were the women's quarters. We stayed against the near wall, not wanting to expose ourselves around the frequent turns, and moved quietly forward. After another hundred feet, I signaled a halt and listened. Laughter, clearly female, could be heard ahead.

"See if there are guards," I whispered to Blue.

He readied his blowgun and was quickly swallowed by the dark corridor. I stared into the space, looking for his figure ahead. Finally I saw a hand waving us forward. We moved together toward a door with two empty chairs beside it. Light came from a crack between the door and the jamb and I went toward it.

The scene was similar to the ribald drawings I had seen from some of the ships we had captured, and I stared for several second before I gained my wits and saw our advantage. With the guards entertained, it would be easy to take them.

The orgy halted and a dozen eyes were on us when we barged through the door. Before the two men could react, Rhames and Swift pulled them away from the women and knocked them out with the butts of the rifles. They lay naked on the floor and I bound them.

The women grabbed for their clothes, but showed no sign of fright. None called for help.

"Pierre sent us," I said in English, hoping someone would understand me.

"Where is he, then?" a voice came from the group. A woman came forward. She was different from the other women; besides her beauty, she carried herself like a queen.

"Are you Cloe?"

She nodded.

"Pierre sent us for you."

Her face changed. "He is alive?"

I could see tears welling in her eyes. "Yes, but the story has to wait. We need your help."

She said something in French and the other girls gathered around. "What is it you need us for?" she asked.

It was a bit of luck to find her and the fact that she spoke English was an added bonus, but not surprising. These islands had changed hands many times over the years and were a true melting pot of cultures. I explained our problem and she translated for the other women.

Off to the side I saw Rhames and Swift enjoying this encounter—each with a girl under each arm. I gave them a stern look, which they acknowledged but didn't move.

"We'll be ready when you need us," Rhames assured me. "But if we've a bit of time …"

The women giggled when he grabbed their breasts and I turned to Blue and Cloe. "Can you take us to his chamber?"

"I can, but I want first shot at the prick," she said.

"So long as we recover the doll and get out of here undetected, he's all yours," I said. She left the room and returned a minute later with a homemade shank.

"I've been waiting for this," she said, brandishing the sharp point.

CHAPTER TWENTY-ONE

The woman led us through a narrow hallway and up a flight of stairs. Swift gladly remained with the other women to ensure none were loyal to Jean-Jean and would set off an alarm. I only hoped he would not be lured in by their charms and miss something.

We stood in front of a locked door. I slid the key ring from my pocket and tried the keys, but this time my luck failed me— none worked. "Anything we do is going to alert the guards," I said, staring at the solid slab of wood.

"It was never locked when Henri was here. Jean–Jean does not call for us. He likes the children," Cloe said.

"Ah, different tastes." I glanced at Rhames to see if he had any ideas.

He removed a pistol he had taken from the guards, placed the tip of the barrel against the lock and cocked the trigger.

"We can't afford the noise," I said. "Let me have that shank," I ordered Cloe.

"I mean to take my revenge on him with it," she said.

"You'll have your chance if we can get in." She handed the homemade blade to me. I took it and placed the sharpened tip in the keyhole. It was narrow enough to fit, but I soon felt resistance. The metal was thin enough that I feared it might snap off inside, foiling any future efforts, and I withdrew it. I worked the blade on the stone wall, making slow passes and watching small filings of the soft metal fall to the ground. I tried it again and it slid in further, but did not reach the mechanism.

"We can't be playing thieves all night," Rhames whispered.

"One more try," I said and began to work the metal against the stone. The shank had a needlelike point now and I went back to the lock. It slid all the way in this time and I wiggled it around trying to feel for the restriction that would free the pins. With my eyes closed I visualized what the key would look like and how it would interact with the mechanism. I pulled it out slightly and turned it again. This would be my only chance. If it failed, the tip of the blade would break off inside the lock.

I felt something move and, with a snap, the lock opened. Rhames quickly moved in front of me and pushed the door open, and the woman leaned over and pulled the blade from the lock. We entered the room and stood side by side, staring at the empty chamber.

"Christ the lord," the woman said. "He's not here."

I looked around the dark room, the only light coming from the moon through the windows. The bed had been slept in. I went to it and put my hand on the sheets—still warm.

"If we'd blown it, we could have taken him by surprise. It was the scratching of the lock that alerted him," Rhames said.

"Search it," I told him, expecting he had taken the doll with him. Until he knew for certain that Pierre was dead I doubted he would let it out of his sight. I started to search the dressing table just in case. "And don't take any prizes."

The double doors leading to the castle burst open and we found ourselves staring at the barrels of half a dozen rifles. Jean-Jean pushed his way between two men of the men, gathering his silk robe around him. The soldiers followed him into the room, staying in a tight semicircle to protect him.

"Take them down to the dungeon," he ordered. "These two, that is. They'll know where Pierre is hiding. The bitch you can take out back and have your way with her. When she's used up —kill her." He went towards the woman and slowly scraped her face with his nail. Blood dripped from the wound, but she did not scream. "Take her before her blood taints the floor," he ordered the guards.

Just before they grabbed her, a flash of light caught my eye and I saw the shank slide from under the folds of her dress. She leaned toward Jean-Jean as if to say something, and waited as he drew close to hear. She whispered again and as he closed the gap to hear her, I saw the razor-sharp blade enter his stomach. He groaned and pulled away, but she held her ground and twisted the shank. He screamed and fell to the ground grabbing his entrails. Rhames pulled the woman back.

"We'll have that doll and be going now," I said and snatched it from his neck.

"It's too late," he said. "I have released him from this world."

Cloe broke free of Rhames's hold, taking all of us by surprise. She lunged across the room, landing the knife in his heart.

The guards stood spellbound, unsure what they should do. I suspected their loyalty may have been forced, but it was not worth the risk. I signaled to Rhames, and we slid behind them, using the brief moment while they stared at Jean-Jean's dead form and wondered what to do. We grabbed their rifles and rendered them unconscious. "Hurry, back the way we came." Already I could hear voices and boots in the hall. I meant to take advantage of the confusion that would ensue.

We ran from the chamber and saw two of the women standing in the doorway staring at the fallen man. They fled ahead of us and we were met by an excited group when we reached the room. They gathered around us, asking what had happened, and if the general was really dead. The mood had changed to one of celebration, but we were reminded of our duty when we heard a gun fire in the hallway. Voices yelled something in French and the women scattered, each seeking refuge behind whatever they could find to conceal them. I heard men coming toward us and looked to Cloe.

She looked me in the eye. "Leave me the rifles and bring Pierre back. We will take care of this." She pushed me toward the door.

I knew better than to argue with a woman once her mind was made up and went for the door. Blue, Rhames and Swift followed me down the hallway, through the gate and into the night. Before we turned off the road, I heard several volleys and could only hope Cloe could handle the situation.

We ran through the night, staying to the road whenever possible, trusting Blue to find our way back to the village. Instead of climbing the road to the Citadel and following the route we had taken, he led us downhill toward the coast. The road ended at a small town near an anchorage. The sun was rising now and we moved off the road to make a plan. We ate some of the food we had pilfered along the way and drank water while we caught our breath, listening for any sign of pursuit.

"We'll be needing a boat anyways," Rhames said. "Might as well take one from here. Those canoes I saw in the village are going to be worthless once we hit real water."

He was right. I looked toward the village and saw a small pier with several craft tied to it. From this spot I could not evaluate them, but any would probably do.

"Take Swift and go. Blue and I will work east away from the village, you can pick us up there." I figured it would look better to have two white men together than the three of us and Blue. I was protective of him ever since the slavers had taken him in Cuba.

Rhames checked his pistol and they moved out. Blue and I went the other way and were soon clear of the town. I was suspicious that there was no pursuit and tried to work the political angles through my mind as we moved. Jean-Jean was clearly hated, as much as if not more than Henri was before him. If Cloe could convince the guards that Pierre was alive and would return, they might be placated. In any event, the paranoid general had left no successors. There would be a power struggle and that would at least give us time to slip away.

I followed Blue down the shore, fingering the doll in my pocket and wondering about its alleged power. Whether it could actually cure him or not, the purported magic put fear in the hearts of the locals. We were on a long section of beach now, the mangroves yielding to the white sand. I went to the water, busy with small boats out fishing and collecting sponges. Without knowing which craft Rhames had taken, we had no choice but to let him find us. I pulled the doll from my pocket and stared at the crude likeness of Pierre. Blue came up beside me, but shied away when he saw the doll.

Suddenly my arm pulsed and Blue jumped back.

"It is the voodoo. It has you now. We must go. It is telling you something."

I thought little of it, attributing the spasm to our exertion and lack of water. Blue was frantic and reached for the doll. He touched it as if it were a child and placed it gently in the pouch he carried.

"You must show it respect," he said. "It is telling you that Pierre is alive and needs our help."

How he'd gathered that I didn't know, but he was resolute. I didn't believe in the magic, but trusted his instincts. With a last glance over my shoulder, we turned inland. I hoped Rhames and Swift would figure it out and wait near the river mouth.

Blue pushed through the brush with a sense of urgency. Where he was normally careful to avoid leaving a trail and often stopped to listen for pursuit, now he blazed a path that even I could follow. His reckoning was right on, though, and we emerged covered in sweat, scrapes and bug bites in the village before noon.

We soon had a crowd around us and Shayla and Red came running from the hut where we had left Pierre. "How is he?"

Before they could answer, the chief pushed through the crowd. "You have the doll?"

Blue looked to me and I nodded. He removed the figure from his pouch and held it with two hands, as if it were a living thing. I reached out to stop him before he could hand it to the chief. "The women first. We have done our part."

He called out and Shayla and Lucy were brought forward. I breathed a sigh of relief. They looked unharmed. My next concern was Pierre. "How is he?"

CHAPTER TWENTY-TWO

Shayla answered. "Much better. He seems no longer to be in pain and the convulsions and fever have passed. The spell remains, though. He has not wakened. The only sign of life we have seen was a peculiar thrashing of his arm this morning."

The chief went to Blue and held out his hand for the doll. I nodded and Blue released it. He took it carefully and studied it. Without a word he walked towards the hut Pierre was being held in.

"Wait. The women. We had a deal," I called out.

He still looked perturbed, but called out to release them. Shayla ran into my arms and I held her tightly, never again wanting to experience the pain of losing her. "There is something else." He turned to look at me. "Jean–Jean is dead. Pierre's woman killed him."

The chief rose and produced a huge bellow of laughter, then went around and slapped us on the back. He seemed to relax now and we followed him to the hut. Pierre was unconscious, but I could see his chest gently rise and fall with his breath. There was no sign of the pain that had previously racked his body. Lucy brewed tea and while we waited for it to cool, we recounted the adventure to the chief. After a few minutes, Lucy tested the dark liquid and slowly poured it into Pierre's mouth.

The chief looked unsettled again and started pacing.

"He says that this will not work. Only the magic he has can help Pierre. We are to follow him. He is ready to conduct the ceremony."

We looked at Lucy, who had just finished pouring the last of the tea into Pierre's mouth. She looked at his face and turned to us with a shrug. "We will see," she said.

The chief seemed anxious and left the hut. We followed him through the village. The cooking fire was blazing, the tips of its flames reaching high into the sky, nearly touching the branches of the overhanging trees. He had the doll in his hand and squatted off to the side, where he opened the crude rendering and removed the nails and hair clippings, carefully handing them to Lucy. Then he started to walk in a circle around the fire, reversing his direction every few revolutions. We could do nothing except stand there and stare at him as he increased his speed and started to chant. The heat was intense and sweat flew from his body as he gyrated around the fire, clutching the doll over his head. The chant turned to a scream and suddenly he threw it into the blaze.

To my amazement the fire hiccupped as if it was about to refuse the doll and sputtered. The chief screamed again and the fire roared back to life.

Exhausted, he came to us. "It is done."

A scream came from the direction of the hut. We left the fire and ran through the village. I expected the worst, but on entering was relieved to find Pierre awake and struggling against the restraints.

Lucy went to him and performed a brief examination. "Release him," she said.

Red and I untied his bonds and he sat up. There was a wild look in his eyes and we all took a step back. Slowly he came under control and collapsed onto the table, asleep. Lucy went to him and wiped his brow.

"He will sleep for a while."

We stood there watching his inert body. Indeed, he appeared to be sleeping peacefully. "When can we move him?"

"Morning," Lucy answered.

She remained in the hut to watch over him and I marveled at her dedication, knowing she had done the same for me after the panther's attack in the grasslands of Florida.

We assembled around the fire, which was slowly dying down to its normal size, and ate from the feast the village had prepared to celebrate the general's death. They passed around gourds, which I assumed contained alcohol, and I had to give stern orders to Red to stay sober.

The group looked at me for direction. "It is late now. If Pierre wakes in the morning as Lucy says, he will either follow us or return to find Cloe. It is his choice. Either way we will head downriver and find Rhames." If there was no treasure to be had here, I wanted off this island.

"Why not just leave now?" Red asked.

"He's part of us, and I won't abandon him like that." That was a bit of the truth, but I also wanted to see if he had any ideas about the treasure. Lucy joined us and said that he had woken, but gone back to sleep. She checked Red's wound and I took the opportunity to take Shayla aside.

We sat together for a while, content just to hold each other, until finally I broke the silence. "What are you thinking?" I asked her.

"I want off this cursed island," she said. "Treasure or not, this is a dangerous place."

"It is," I agreed. "Rhames and Swift should have a boat in the river mouth. Tomorrow morning we will find them."

"What about Pierre?" she asked.

I thought for a moment. "He's part of the crew, but it is his choice. Cloe is back at the palace and I suspect the opportunity to take power will probably keep him here."

"But if there is no treasure, he will not have a chance."

I looked at her, surprised by her political acumen. "I hadn't thought of that, but it's his decision either way." I was about to pull her closer, but was interrupted by a call from the clearing.

"He is awake," Lucy called out.

We jumped up and went to the hut. Pierre was sitting up now, drinking tea. "It is good to see you, my friend," I said.

"And you as well," he responded, his voice hoarse.

Shayla spoke something to him but all I could make out was Cloe's name. At the mention of her he smiled and then looked at me.

"He wants to know what has happened," Shayla said.

I looked at him watching me. I left nothing out, pausing only to answer his questions.

"So, he is dead?" he asked.

I nodded.

"And Cloe has remained?" he asked.

"Yes, she seemed to think you would understand her reasons."

He sat up straighter and I could sense his authority. The

silence grew uncomfortable while we waited for him to answer.

"There is no way to take control without the gold. We may be able to hold off the president in the South, but not for long," he said. He looked deflated.

"And there are no other clues to where the treasure was taken?" I asked, not sure that I wanted the answer if it lay anywhere in this country.

"I will speak to the chief. He knows this island and can tell me what he has heard since I was sold into slavery," Pierre said.

He got up and took a few tentative steps.

"We plan to leave in the morning," I said.

"I will have information and a decision by then," Shayla translated and he walked out of the hut.

"Tell him that we will join him." We were equal partners and had gone through considerable pains to get here. I did not want to be undermined and have the treasure taken from us. We walked together back to the fire past incredulous looks and dropped draws as the villagers saw Pierre fully healed. The chief was still by the fire.

"Don't interpret. Just the important parts," I told Shayla and we sat down.

After an extended conversation that seemed to be amongst old friends, Shayla whispered in my ear. "He says we were closer before."

"What do you mean?"

"This dialect is strange to me, but from what I can gather, it seems that Henri became ever more paranoid before his death. There are rumors that he had the treasure removed from the island and taken north."

"Great Inagua?" I asked.

She nodded.

The chief rose a few minutes later. "And what is your decision?" I asked Pierre. There was light in the sky now and I wanted to move out.

"I cannot take this country without a treasury. If you are willing we will go back to the Bahamas and find this gold."

I was already getting anxious about our ships and the treasure. "And then?"

"He asks that you provide him transport back to Haiti."

I agreed. If he was able to take the island it might be a safe refuge—away from the Americans and British who both sought us.

The sky was lighter now and we went back to the hut to rouse the others. The chief hugged Pierre before we left and gave us two canoes with his warriors to guide us to the mouth of the river. Once there I hoped we would find Rhames and signal the *Caiman*.

We set off in a convoy of four canoes, with several of his warriors in each to navigate the river. Its course took us through several sections of rapids. The smaller ones we rode through, the larger we portaged around. By nightfall we landed on a beach by the ocean.

I searched the horizon for any sign of Rhames, but the boats fishing on the reef line a quarter mile offshore all looked the same. I guessed that if we couldn't see him, we would be invisible as well. We had lost the bundle of Chinese rockets somewhere in the brush and I sought for a way to signal him. I paced along the beach, staring at the boats, and upon turning, I ran straight into the pirate.

"Bloody hell would I like to get off this cursed island,"

Rhames said.

We clapped each other on the back. "What about a boat?"

"Aye, the natives are a bit prickly," he said.

Reunited by whatever stroke of luck, we needed to signal Mason, but without the flares, he would never know it was us. I put the question to the group and Pierre responded.

"He says there is a substance they used on the sugar plantations that will light the sky when mixed with powder."

I wasn't sure what he was talking about, but Rhames seemed interested.

Pierre got up and touched Blue on the shoulder. "He says they will be back by midnight. Something about a sugar beet plantation not far from here." Shayla shrugged. "I have no ideas what he means."

"You should take Rhames and Swift for protection," I offered.

He shook his head. "He says they walk like oafs."

They left and we settled in to wait. I used the opportunity to lay out our supplies and weapons. Rhames and Swift helped clean the guns while Shayla sorted out our food stores. Lucy took Red back to the river to clean his wound. We packed everything in palm fronds, anticipating a wet exit from the country, and settled in to wait.

The moon was high in the sky when they returned, but by the look on their faces I knew they had been successful. Pierre came forward and laid out a pile of a chalklike substance they had packed in a piece of cloth.

We gathered around like it was something precious, and it was —I recognized it at once as saltpeter.

I debated whether to start the fire now, and saw no downside.

With Jean-Jean dead, the military would be in disarray and I doubted anyone was looking for us. Besides, if they did find us, we were well armed and ready. I asked Rhames to set up our defenses in case we drew in the wrong people and went with Blue and Pierre to start a fire.

With all the wood still soaked from the rain, it was harder than I'd expected. While we waited for the wet timbers to dry and catch, Rhames dumped a handful of black powder onto the sputtering flames, which quickly ignited the wood. The flames were high in the sky now and I saw Rhames looking around the camp. He had combined the saltpeter and the remainder of our powder.

"We need something round and hollow," he said.

There was nothing I could think of that would fit his description and I was about to give up when Blue took one of their blowguns and, using a sharp rock, cut it into half a dozen pieces. In each he packed the powder, then took a stick and hollowed out the middle.

One at time he tossed the tubes onto the fire. For a long minute we stood staring at the flames in defeat. Nothing in this country had gone as planned; why should we expect our exit to be any different? I turned away, trying to come up with any other way to signal Mason, when the fire sputtered. Hoping for the best, I turned around, but the flame died down. I looked away again and stared at the ocean, hoping for the sight of a sail in the moonlight, when the second tube blew. This time it launched a few feet in the air before sputtering. The other tubes did the same and my hope died with them.

CHAPTER TWENTY-THREE

Rhames had not given up, though. I noticed he had gathered some seaweed and set it close to the fire. He then pulled some embers out and scooped them into a shell with a stick. We were all watching him now as he took some of the dried seaweed and placed it in another shell. He was intent on what he was doing and a rare smile crossed his battle-worn face. Despite our situation, I could tell he was enjoying himself. With a small rock he ground the two substances. Once he had a quantity of each, he mixed the seaweed, charcoal and saltpeter together, carefully judging the color before adjusting the proportions.

"Mind the ladies," he said, turning to the mixture and urinating on it. "Works like a charm," he laughed and turned back to us. He took the paste and spread it on several green palm fronds, setting them a safe distance from the fire, but still within range of its heat.

I left the group and went to the water's edge. It was low tide and the wet sand felt good on my bare feet. Shayla came up beside me and together we stared out to sea.

"Do you think they saw it?" she asked.

I was careful not to inflict my pessimism on her. "We won't

know till morning. He won't chance an approach in the dark." I moved backwards as a large wave crashed at my feet. There were still a few hours until sunrise and together we walked back to the camp to find a place to rest. Rhames, Blue and Pierre were busy by the fire. They had collected several large conch shells and stuffed them full of the mixture and were about to throw them on the fire.

"Stop! Those are bombs," I said.

"Bloody right they are," Rhames said proudly.

My spirit had ebbed, but not enough to watch him blow us up. "Wait for the dawn and if he doesn't show, we'll give it a shot." I waited until they had backed away from the fire before moving to where Shayla sat by a large palm tree. I tried to rest, but sleep eluded me. I couldn't sit still.

"What is it?" Shayla murmured, half-asleep.

"No worries, get some rest," I said and walked towards the brush. Rhames's crude bombs had given me an idea. The tubes we had tried earlier were a step in the right direction; they were just not the right projectiles. It was hard going in the dark, especially not being sure what I was looking for. With sweeping motions, I scoured the brush, looking for anything that was hollow, or could easily be whittled out. Sharp leaves cut my arms and mosquitos swarmed around my face as I moved inland. I continued forward and stumbled into a small salt marsh. The reeds snapped in my hands when I grabbed them for support and I looked at the hollowed-out section of the broken stem. I quickly gathered as many as I could carry and ran back to the fire.

I set them down and one at a time cut the reeds into foot-long pieces, using a small stalk to hollow out the centers, then sharpened one end and filled them with powder. Rhames saw what I was doing and came over to help. He dragged several embers from the main fire and started a smaller blaze a few feet away. The first rays of the sun were in the sky now and we needed to move fast to gain the maximum effect if the rockets actually worked. We moved our possessions to the water's edge and gathered together.

"Who's it going to be?" I asked, looking for a volunteer.

"You'll not let me miss this," Rhames answered and went to the fire before anyone else could speak.

The rest of us stood by the water, what we hoped was a safe distance from the fires. Rhames took the first stalk, jammed the sharpened end into the smaller fire and jumped back. Nothing happened and he was about to reach his hand in when with a burst, the stalk shot into the air, leaving a trail of sparks behind it. He hooted like a child and set two more in the fire. The first rocket reached its apex and exploded, showering sparks behind it.

He set off the remaining rockets two at a time. When he was finished we stood together on the shore watching for any sign of a ship. If Mason had not seen the display, he was nowhere near. I turned away after a few minutes, not wanting to think of our options if he hadn't seen the flares.

"There!" Swift yelled. "There she is!"

A ship showed on the horizon, clearly moving toward the beach. We watched as the shape of the *Caiman* became visible. Under full sail, she came within a quarter mile of the beach and hove to. The skiff was dropped and several men climbed in. Within minutes they were on the beach, but a gunshot tore my attention from our rescuers. Down the beach, a band of uniformed soldiers kneeled in the sand and fired. We hit the beach just in time and the bullets flew over our heads. More men were coming toward us. Obviously our rockets had been seen by our enemies as well.

"Into the skiff," I ordered and waited for them to load up. "Everyone in. Go!"

"What about you?" Rhames called.

"I'll swim." Before they could hesitate I ran toward the fire, turning back to make sure they had pushed off. They were in the swells now, working hard to get past the breakers before they were swamped. I moved to the far side of the fire, hoping it obscured me from the attackers' view. They were split into two groups now, one reloading to fire on the skiff, the other running toward me. I grabbed the shells that Rhames had made, hoping they would actually work, and moved to the edge of the brush. I heard a round of gunfire and looked out at the skiff bobbing in the calmer water beyond the surf. I could see the bullets hit the water just short of them. The men ran forward, shortening the angle of their shot, and started to reload. The skiff was in range now and I had to act.

I left the cover of the brush and threw two of the shells into the fire. Not knowing what to expect, I dove back into the brush for cover and waited. Seconds later the first bomb blew up, scattering burning branches and red-hot embers a hundred feet in each direction. I brushed the sparks off myself and watched the soldiers scatter and run for cover when the second round blew, throwing more embers after them. In their haste they had run right past me. I waited a few seconds and ran for the surf.

Someone yelled behind me and several shots fired. To escape

them, I dove into a wave, staying underwater for as long as I could. I surfaced briefly and swam hard for the *Caiman*. They fired another round and I chanced a look back at the beach. Seeing I was out of range, I eased my stroke. The soldiers stood in a line on the beach staring at me.

I reached the ladder and climbed aboard. Within seconds, Mason had ordered the ship to come about and slowly the *Caiman* turned and headed out to sea. I wasn't sure who else had seen the fireworks, and I'd had enough action for one day. The sooner we were over the horizon, the better I would feel.

Mason adjusted the course and the sails filled with the wind. We were moving now and I started to relax as the beach faded from view. Exhausted, I collapsed on the deck.

Someone handed me a mug of water. The sweet rainwater tasted good after inhaling more salt water than I would have liked on my swim out. Finally I had enough energy to rise and went to the helm.

Mason and Rhames were there looking at the chart. "It was there the whole time?" I heard Mason ask him.

They made room for me and together we looked at Great Inagua. "Where do you think it is?"

I went to find Pierre. He was in my cabin with Shayla. The logbook was in front of them, but they were focused on each other. My blood started to boil when she touched his elbow and they both shared a smile. I cleared my throat and spoke, trying to hide my irritation. "We'll be needing a destination."

He didn't look up, but turned his attention to the book, glancing back at the chart every few seconds, shaking his head as if nothing had just happened. He spoke again and I wished there was someone else to translate. The two were too close for my liking.

"He says there are two reefs on the south side of the island. A northwest heading will get you close," she said.

I went back to the helm and relayed the instructions to Mason. He set the watch and Red took the wheel.

"How's the arm?" I asked, noticing the small piece of cloth still wrapped around it.

"Pretty close to healed now, thanks to that woman," he said and swung the wheel to our new course, calling to the men in the rigging to adjust the sails to a broad reach.

We settled in for what I hoped was an easy and uneventful passage. Finally the tips of the high mountains vanished below the horizon and I went down to my cabin. Pierre and Shayla were still there, but at least they appeared to be working out a math problem on the table.

"Can we talk?" I asked Shayla.

She turned to Pierre and said something that made him laugh. It was all I could do to control myself when she touched his arm when he rose.

"What's with you and the Haitian?"

She turned to look at me. "His name is Pierre. What's bothering you?"

She had asked it as if there was nothing wrong. I was flustered now and the words sputtered from my mouth. "The two of you. Your secrets and looks and …"

"Oh, sweet Jesus, is that it?" she laughed.

"Don't dismiss me like that," I said.

She rose and faced me. "Dear Nick, it's his woman, Cloe. That's what we talk about. I didn't think you'd want to hear about his personal affairs." She stepped forward.

I felt the fool but didn't know what to do. Backing down too easily made me look weak, and my jealous fit had already embarrassed me. She seemed to sense my dilemma.

"At first he was concerned and told me about their meeting and life together. Now he is just happy."

She leaned into me and I felt her tongue in my mouth. Before I could say anything we were on the bunk.

CHAPTER TWENTY-FOUR

I woke with a start sometime in the middle of the night. Lying in bed, I tried to go back to sleep, but the riddle of the chart and the logbook ran through my mind. Shayla snored quietly next to me, and it took an effort to leave her.

I went on deck and relieved myself, staring into the night sky and wondering how to unravel the clues the French captain had left. Swift had the watch, and I went to the wheel, where we exchanged a few words. He gave me our location and I looked into the rigging to make sure the sails were reefed. The wind had shifted during the previous day, moving to the north, forcing us to tack in order to make headway. The maneuvers delayed us, but I expected we would make landfall sometime in the late morning.

I said goodnight and went down to the cabin, where I lit a lantern, placing it so the light was focused on the table, though just enough bled onto Shayla so I could see her form. I looked over and smiled at her clinging to the pillow where I had just lain, an impish grin on her face.

I pulled the logbook and paper toward me. There were some rudimentary angles drawn on the scratch paper, but I immediately knew they were wrong. My eyelids were heavy, and I had nodded off twice in the chair before I decided to take a break. "Maybe if I get some sleep it will come," I said quietly to myself so as not to wake her, and I collapsed on the bunk next to her.

As I lay there it dawned on me that people did their dreaming on charts. I remembered some of the old charts Gasparilla had shown me with dragons and sea monsters marking the unknown. The logbook, on the other hand, was a historical record of where the ship had been and what they had done. The answer had to be on the chart still unfolded on the table.

Giving up on sleep, I rubbed my eyes and rose, careful not to wake Shayla. I went to the table and stared at it again, this time certain it had the answer. I shook my head at the X on the island of Haiti, that I now knew marked the Citadel and a dead end. I looked past the obvious navigational notes that didn't apply to the treasure and focused on the two items that didn't relate to anything. The first was the straight line seemingly placed randomly to the west of Haiti. I set the ruler on the compass rose and adjusted it until it paralleled the line. It read thirteen degrees, but I had no idea how this related to anything. The second item was the gibberish written on the bottom. *Yr geéfbe fr gebbir ra qrffbhf qr yn fhesnpr ceéf qr yn cbvagr yn cyhf frcgragevbanyr fhe yr pôgé bhrfg.*

I stared at the letters, trying to figure out what language they were written in, but the words made no sense in any language I was familiar with. Setting the strange words aside, I looked at Great Inagua. With a ruler I laid out our present course and discovered it looked like it would intersect the line. On a whim I placed the ruler over the old line and extended it to the north. It ran straight through the island. I leaned back trying to figure out the significance of what I had just discovered, but aside from telling me we were moving in the right direction, it told me nothing. It could be thirteen degrees from anywhere. I followed the line to its southern extremity and found it originated at Cartagena, near the northern tip of South America.

The captain's logbook would tell me if they had ever visited the pirate stronghold. I opened the book, leaned back in the chair and started to skim through the pages. I didn't have to look far. There were several pages and drawings near the front of the book. I studied the captain's writing, not understanding the words, but looking for the name of places and anything that related to thirteen degrees, but came up empty. The entries were mechanical, stating the provisions they had acquired and an accounting of the supplies. Nothing seemed out of place. I turned the pages, scanning the remaining entries to see where they had gone next, and found a missing page. It was not apparent at first, having been cut from the spine with a knife rather than torn. The following page placed them hear Honduras—a substantial gap.

I moved forward, plotting their journey up the Mexican coast and across the Caribbean, but nowhere did thirteen degrees come in. Flipping back, I looked at the page numbers and noticed the missing page was thirteen. There had to be a significance to the number but I had no idea what it was. From Cartagena they had traveled northwest and then east across the Caribbean. The logbook showed no course at thirteen degrees. Superstition could be at play, but why mark the line on the chart?

I had to look forward and not back if I was to figure out the riddle. The chart had markings all over it and I found a light line marking the ship's passage from South America to where we had taken her. There were other lines and notes as well, but they were in a different hand and I expected they were from the previous captain.

The strange phrase caught my eye again. They were clearly words and I realized that if they were not in any language prevalent in this hemisphere, it was likely a code. Gasparilla had used ciphers before to communicate with other captains, most notably Lafitte. I was fully alert now, looking on the letters in a new light.

Knowing what it was and breaking the cipher were two different matters. There were two kinds of codes that we had used before, but I discounted the method where identical books were used by people in different locations, an agreed-on page and line revealing the key. The other method was simpler but had multiple combinations. It would be tedious, but I had a good feeling it was a Cesarian code. The cipher was based on advancing the alphabet by a set number of characters.

I pulled out a blank piece of paper and made a chart showing the progression of letters and numbers and started working through them. There were a few close calls, but none made it past the first four letters. I sat back and rubbed my eyes, dreading the work ahead. It could take hours to work through the combinations. I looked back down at the chart and saw the line again.

Thirteen had some significance to the captain. I laid out the alphabets with A starting under the thirteenth letter N. I wrote down an L on the paper and looked up the next letter. After the first three words I knew I was on the right track. I didn't understand the words, but suspected they were French. It took the better part of an hour to finish the translation and I looked down on the paper and read the words in my head: *Le trésor se trouve en dessous de la surface près de la pointe la plus septentrionale sur le côté ouest.*

I looked over at Shayla, still sleeping peacefully and went to her. "Wake up. I need you." I shook her shoulder.

She opened one eye and smiled. "I need you too, but in the morning if it still suits you," she said and closed her eye.

"No, I have it."

"Good for you, now let me sleep." She rolled over and faced the bulkhead.

"Please. Just a minute and you can go back to sleep."

She rolled back over and looked at me. "You always say that," she said.

I went for the paper and handed it to her.

"What's that, then?" she asked, leaning on an elbow as she read it.

"Can you translate it for me?" I asked.

She was fully awake now and sat up. "This is it!" One word at a time, she read it in French and then translated it into English: *The treasure can be found below the surface near the northernmost tip on the west side.*

I hugged her and took the paper, writing down the English translation. She was wide awake now and pulled a shift over her head, then ran her fingers through her hair. Together we left the cabin and climbed to the deck. It was still dark, but the sky to the east held the glow of the sun just below the horizon. Swift had given the helm to Mason when the watch changed several hours before, and I followed the glow of his pipe to where he sat.

"Here it is!" I handed him the paper with the code and translation. "This should get us within spitting distance of the king's gold."

"And just in time. We should make landfall any time now."

He lashed the wheel and we went to the chart, taking the translation with him. "There's the northern tip," he said, pointing to it with his finger.

There was no mistaking the point sticking out far to the north of the rest of the island. "And to the west puts it here." I pointed to the side of the landmass of Little Inagua.

"It says it's below the surface. Do you reckon that means water or land?" he asked.

"Only one way to find out, but the diving gear is on the *Panther.*" There had been no need to take it with us.

"Best to see what things look like before we go messing with the magistrate. After last time, we don't want no one tagging along," he said and went back to the wheel, where he released the line holding the spokes and turned to the east.

CHAPTER TWENTY-FIVE

We stood by the helm, the original pirates, Mason and I. Pierre and Shayla stood off to the side. They were close enough that she could translate what was being said, but stood so they were not included in any decision. Shayla as yet had no vote, something that still weighed on my mind. I hoped they saw her in a different light now after her help in Haiti.

"So, you're sure you have this right?" Rhames asked.

I laid the paper with the translation over the chart. "It's similar to the code Gasparilla used," I said, trying to use our mentor's name to give it more credibility. "Julius Caesar used it as well."

"I don't know about Julius bloody Caesar, but if it worked for the captain I would believe it."

I had explained my process in solving the clues left by the French captain and pointed to the northernmost point of the island. "The clues lead here."

"Be nice to have a local to guide us. Ain't no telling about the reefs and there's bound to be some tricky currents with structures like that," Mason said.

I couldn't disagree with his reasoning. The arrows on the

chart showing the path of the Gulf Stream were very close to the eastern edge of the island and we had seen just how deadly the reefs could be in the Caymans. "I thought about going back to town, but the magistrate'll see us come into the harbor. I don't want any interference like last time. Besides, I'm not all that trusting of him after he took Pott."

They all nodded. "So we are in agreement?"

"Aye," Rhames said with Swift and Red concurring. "Let's go have a look."

It was still hard for the old pirates to see into the future. Speculation was not in their blood. They were not used to plans and explorations that might not yield any result. Stalking the shipping lanes with the lure of a sail on the horizon had been as much planning as they cared for. We were in sight of land and adjusted our course to take us around the less populated eastern side of the island. I went to where Pierre and Shayla stood.

"So you heard, then?" I asked.

"But why not go back for the other ship and go together? I'd like to know my father's all right," she said. "Maybe he knows this area."

I hadn't thought that Phillip might have sailed these waters. Things change quickly in these latitudes. "I'd like to get the gold without anyone else knowing if possible. Then we'll go back for the other ship and take the temperature of the colony," I said.

I went down to my cabin and lay down on the bunk, exhausted after being up all night, knowing that we had several hours before we would reach the likely spot.

***

* * *

The sun was just starting its decline in the western sky when I rose and went back on deck, feeling refreshed after a few hours' sleep. I went to the port rail and looked out at the island—just another atoll in the Caribbean. It was odd how some of the islands had hills and mountains and others, like this one, were low and barren.

Ahead I could see what I thought was the northern tip and went to the helm to confirm our position.

"Be around it in an hour or so," Mason said from the wheel. "I'm hoping for a nice anchorage in the lee."

"I'll get the chart from below and see if there are any markings." I went to the cabin and rolled up the French captain's chart. Back on deck, I laid it over the larger one Mason was using.

"So there's the mysterious line," he said, studying the captain's marks.

I focused on the island itself, but there were no notes or any indication the Frenchman had knowledge of this area.

"See how his line goes to that small point there." He pointed to a small spit of land. "The line's not there by accident. I'd guess that'd be the best place to start."

I agreed, becoming less sure of our goal after looking at the long coastline. We had to start somewhere, and it had to yield results or Rhames, Red and Swift would lose interest. Without immediate gratification they would become unruly and hinder the search. "Right then. That's where we'll start."

Mason had what he needed and I climbed into the rigging to get a better look at the coastline. We gave the island plenty of leeway, staying a mile from shore. The features on the land were indistinguishable from this distance, but the water to starboard was an indigo color and the long swells told me we were skirting the Gulf Stream. There was a distinct line of small waves and debris where the current clashed with the shallower water. It was alive with flying fish springing from the bow remaining in the air for what looked like a hundred feet before reentered the water. I heard Blue and Lucy below, howling with excitement as they brought in several small dolphinfish. To the north, a smaller island was visible on the horizon. My mind started to wander, speculating about the treasure and what we would do after we found it. It would have to be large to satisfy everyone after Pierre and the crown took their share.

A call from below brought me back to reality. Men scurried up the rigging beside me and I heard Mason call out an order to change the sails. We were moving past the center of the wind and he was preparing to jibe. With a less skilled man at the helm, this was a dangerous maneuver, but Mason had a feel for these things. He waited until we were in the middle of the channel between the two islands and slowly started a turn to port. Many inexperienced sailors will rush this move, causing the sails to slam across, often throwing the men from the rigging, but Mason eased across the wind, calling out the exact moment when the booms would swing. With barely a sound the sails swung over as he continued his turn.

The island was on our port side now, the water a much lighter blue and the land vacant. We were close-hauled, pointing into the wind when he called to drop half the canvas. With the island blocking the wind, the seas were flat and I could see every detail of the bottom through the clear water. Swift went to the bowsprit with the lead and started calling readings back to Mason. I turned my gaze to the land and saw a building still under construction. The call was three fathoms and Mason ordered the sails furled. A few minutes later the anchor dropped and the ship swung and settled.

I climbed down, excited to start the search. Shayla was on deck now and together we went to meet the men at the helm.

"The clue says underneath, but it don't say whether it's the water or the land. Look over there." Rhames pointed to the building. "Could be there, here or anywhere. Bloody treasure hunting," he grumbled.

Pierre turned to the building I had seen and said something. We were so used to Shayla translating now that we didn't even look at her. "He says that Henri had started to build this retreat here in case he was deposed."

That gave us some hope we were in the right place. "We still have a few hours of light left. Why don't we split up? Rhames, take Red, Swift and Blue. Check out the building site. Mason and I will see what lies beneath us." Looking at the expanse of water and land, my excitement waned. The closer we were to the treasure, the farther away it seemed. The area was too vast. There had to be another clue to narrow our search.

Rhames armed the men and they climbed into the skiff. They were soon on the beach and making for the building. I turned to Mason, not able to hide the smile on my face. Remembering the stunning dives off the Caymans, I wanted nothing more than to get back underwater, but that would have to wait. With no idea where the treasure might lay, I had to find another clue.

Mason and I stared at the chart and my confidence waned further. There were no other clues that would put us closer. I called for Shayla and Pierre to interpret the writing, wanting as many eyes and viewpoints as we could get.

The four of us gathered around the table and Pierre moved carefully around the chart, translating the writing. It all seemed inconsequential. Shayla stepped in.

"It says on the west side of the northernmost tip, right?" Shayla asked and leaned in. "Show me the spot."

Mason set the straight edge facing east and west at the very tip of land. Shayla was about to say something when we all saw it. To be sure, Mason drew a light line where the straight edge lay and then moved it to the thirteen-degree line, extending it until they intersected. We looked out at the water imagining the spot and saw nothing but blue water.

"It'll be too deep there," Mason said. "It's something else."

"Henri would never put it so close to his retreat," Pierre said.

"But look here," Shayla continued with her own thoughts. "How close the line is to the small island."

We looked at what was just a dot on the map. It was so small that I had ignored it, but now, as we looked north, we could see the island in the distance. "That may be it. If I were a paranoid man, that is where I would hide it. Still in sight, but far removed."

I knew the line would be less than accurate; with an island this small and the questionable precision of the charts it could be off by a mile. I dared not get excited, but when I extended the thirteen-degree line the intersection was just west of the tip. I looked at the sun and cursed that there was not enough daylight to search that day. Gunshots came from the beach and we all ran to the deck.

CHAPTER TWENTY-SIX

We ran to the rail and saw a flurry of activity on shore. Rhames and the men were running back to the skiff with a larger group in pursuit. More shots were fired and I saw a man drop. Our men were behind the skiff, using it for cover, but they were under siege. The other men had taken positions and would attack the minute Rhames made a move.

"Quick, get the guns ready," I yelled to the men. With three crewmen I ran to the capstan and we hauled the anchor in. Next I turned to Mason. "Get us underway. They're pinned down, we have to help." He called out the orders to the remaining crew and I felt the boat shift. "Take her around," I told him and went to the guns. With Rhames trapped on shore it was my responsibility to check the loads and site the cannon.

The *Caiman* started to move and I waited for Mason to pick his line. Shallow water was clearly visible about a hundred yards off the beach, and I would have to wait until we turned to make the final adjustments. I looked back to land and saw a volley come from our men, but their attackers were dug in. It would remain a standoff until Rhames ran out of ammunition—then they would be overrun.

The sails started to fill and Mason adjusted our course to catch the wind. We were too close to the shallows and he turned away from the shore, executing a quick jibe in order to gain enough leeway to come about and make a run by the beach. The ship veered slightly and he called out the command. The *Caiman* moved easily through the wind and settled onto a port tack. I waited until she settled on her new course and reset the elevation screws on the starboard carronades. Slowly we crept by the beach and I gauged the time and distance before calling the order to fire.

The *Caiman* rocked back as her guns fired. "Swing around in case we need to use the port guns," I said to Mason and climbed partway up the rope ladder by the mainmast to see what damage we had caused. Rhames and the men had used the covering fire to put the skiff to sea, and the men were pulling hard toward us. Mason saw them and adjusted course to intercept. Shots came from the beach, but the skiff was already out of range.

With the sails backed to the wind we waited for them to come alongside us. The minute the skiff was secure, I called to Mason to set course for Little Inagua. I had no idea what the men on the beach were about, and suspecting the treasure was on the smaller island, there was no reason to stay and find out.

Rhames was first over the rail, and I took him and Pierre aside for his report. "What happened?" I asked.

"I can't tell you if the gold's there," he said, trying to catch his breath. "But about twenty of them have a camp set up and are digging all 'round that half-finished house." He took another few breaths. "From the look of them, they've been at it awhile with no result."

I turned to Rhames. "Any sign of a ship?"

"Just a few of the native canoes. I'd guess they came overland. There was some carts around for their equipment, and donkeys to pull them." He looked forward. "Where're we heading?"

I told him about our new theory and he just shook his head and walked away, muttering something about pirating being an easier business. We were approaching the smaller island now and I went back to the helm.

"It's going to be too dangerous in this light," Mason said.

I looked at the sun, now only four fingers above the horizon. With just an hour of daylight, I agreed. "Just get in the lee and we'll find an anchorage. Far enough up the coast so they can't see our masts."

He turned to port. With the wind behind us we had an easy run across the narrow channel and started to move up the coast. This part of the island was nothing more than a salt marsh, barely a foot out of the water, providing no cover. Flamingos lined the shores, mocking us as we passed, somehow knowing they were protected by the reefs surrounding the island.

We were close to the tip now with no suitable anchorage in sight. Flamingos continued to line the shores and I heard a strange sound, much like the braying of donkeys. I took the glass and went into the rigging. With my forearms braced between the lines I scanned the island. There were indeed donkeys and goats, but no sign of man. I could almost smell roast goat, and planned to send Rhames on a hunting party once we were anchored.

The landscape started to change as we approached the tip of the island. A layer of hardpan was visible on the shoreline, rising slightly from the water. Small coves dotted the coast, but as inviting as they were, we would be unable to cross the reef to reach them.

I climbed down and went back to the helm. "Nothing," I said to Mason. "How do you feel about anchoring out here?"

"Not well. The swell's troubling. One big roller and the anchor'd pull, sending us into the reef. I'm thinking we need to reef the sails and stay offshore overnight."

He was right, and I tried to put the roast goat dinner from my mind. Taking station off the coast would tax the crew, but it was the only course open to us. "Right then. Set the watch," I said and left the deck.

Shayla was in the cabin, reading through the logbook. "Going to dive in the morning?" she asked.

"The pump's on the *Panther*," I answered. "I was hoping to find the spot and see what we could under our own air." I lay down on the bunk and, as I was just about asleep, I felt her next to me.

"Let me go with you. They say that women have better air than men." She jokingly jabbed me with her elbow and smiled. "I've got some skill here. Spent many an afternoon after school on the reefs around the harbor gathering sponges and spearing fish."

I didn't want to think about endangering her again after just escaping from Haiti. I merely nodded and stopped the conversation by leaning in and nuzzling her breasts.

***

The morning air was heavy with humidity; small puffy clouds, the harbinger of the large thunderstorms I feared would develop, were already present in the sky. The deck was quiet, the men on watch, resting against the gunwales. Having to stand off the coast all night had forced Mason to split the crew into thirds, leaving enough men on deck at any one time to maneuver the ship. The result was that no one had gotten a full night's sleep. Swift was at the helm and we stood together. "Going to be stormin' later," he said.

I looked back at the sky. "Best get to the work quickly. Call the watch," I said and went to the forepeak. He yelled an order and the men on deck came to their feet. Swift sent them to the rigging and waited for the rest of the crew to come up. The island was still a mile off. I heard the order to come about and grabbed a line as the bow swung into the waves and crossed the wind. Behind me I heard Mason's voice and went back to the helm. Rhames was by his side.

"What's our plan?" he asked, sweat already on his brow from the thick air.

"Get as close to the spot we marked and have a look. Then we'll decide," I said.

I sensed the restlessness of the crew. After our failed attempt in Haiti, they were getting anxious, and the action last night was doing nothing to ease their nerves. I knew their minds: If they were to face bullets and steel, they might as well know the prize before they took the risk.

"My guess is it's right there," Mason said, pointing to a small cove off the tip of the island. "Waves're breaking a good ways out. I don't reckon we can get too close."

"Do the best you can and we'll take the skiff in." I left him, went to the foremast and climbed to the topsail spar. From this height I could see the sand through the clear water and heard six fathoms called from the bow. I looked ahead and saw the cove, a perfect horseshoe ringed by rock. A reef guarded its entry, whitewater breaking on the exposed coral, showing its teeth. If that's where it was, he had chosen well, I thought, trying to figure the best way in. Fortunately the tide was on the rise and might allow just enough water over the reef for the skiff.

I climbed down and had a few words with Mason before selecting the men I knew to be good with the skiff to make up my crew. Mason called for the sails to be furled and the *Caiman* crept toward the reef. The current was against the wind, leaving us almost stationary, and we dropped anchor in four fathoms, about a quarter mile from our goal.

I approached Shayla and told her my decision to take her and we joined the four others waiting by the ladder.

"What's with the girl?" Rhames asked. "This ain't no place for a lovers' picnic." He laughed at his joke.

"She's a strong swimmer, might be some use to us." Before I could continue my argument, she pulled her shift over her head and dove off the rail. She had done this once before and I was not overly worried, but as we gathered by the rail there was no sign of her.

It seemed like minutes had elapsed and a crowd had gathered around us, each man pressing forward, watching the water for any sign of her. I was past worry now and stripped my shirt off and dove in after her. I hit the water and started clawing my way down, refusing to blink or I might miss her. After only seconds, my lungs burned and I was about to surface when suddenly a shape shot gracefully past me. I surfaced just after her and heard the men cheer as she held a conch shell over her head.

We swam to the ladder and boarded the ship. I was about to

scold her for the stunt when Rhames took her hand to help her on deck.

"Four fathoms is better than any man I've seen," he spoke in approval.

***

There were six of us in the skiff: Shayla, three crewmen, Rhames and myself. Rhames had insisted on accompanying us in case there was any threat from the land. With the flood tide, the reef lay submerged now, but I knew it was there. The men at the oars held water while I counted the waves, waiting for the three larger ones that always came together. The first one passed under the skiff, raising it in the water, and I yelled for them to row. The small boat picked up momentum, and on the crest of the third wave we coasted over the reef.

We sat in the small cove now, the water so clear that I could see fish swimming up to the hull. A small herd of goats taunted Rhames from the small bluff and he looked at me for permission to shoot one. "Later. Let's get in the water before the storms hit." I looked to the sky and couldn't help but notice the small clouds were now larger, their bottoms becoming dark and heavy with moisture.

With the threat of weather, we rolled off the side of the skiff and dove, the piece of lead we each held effortlessly dragging us to the bottom. I waited until Shayla was by my side before proceeding. It was deep enough to make my ears pop and I barely reached the sandy bottom on my first try. I dropped the lead, but held the line secured to it as I went back to the surface for air. With this system we could use the weight to pull ourselves down, saving energy and air. We took turns diving until I felt the first drop of rain. It was discouraging, finding nothing but sand.

"We're done," I said to Rhames and climbed aboard. "If you hurry, you can take a goat." He smiled at this and helped the men aboard. Shayla swam to me. I grabbed her arm and lifted her over the gunwale. The look on her face mirrored my disappointment. Rhames rowed to the shore and we beached the skiff on the rocks. He climbed out, staying low to the ground, and crept to the small bluff.

"I saw nothing but sand," Shayla said.

The other men were saying much the same thing. "It has to be here," I said. "The line runs right through the cove. If I only had the gear, I could really scout it out." It dawned on me as soon as I said the words. Henri's men would not have had pumps and gear. With a treasure as heavy as it was reported, they would have had to work in shallower water. I looked at the bluffs and saw a small opening.

"Come on." I grabbed her hand and led her around the cove. When we reached the spot I had seen, I eased myself over the rock face, landing in chest-deep water. There was what looked like a cave, carved out of the rock by the tides, and she followed me as I swam toward it. It was dark inside, with only a foot of air above our heads, and I felt for the bottom. Instead of finding the sand, I slid into the water, swallowing a mouthful when my head submerged.

I resurfaced and spat out the water I had inhaled. We were both treading water and I didn't want to waste any energy with too much talk. "It's another hole."

"Let me try," she said.

I nodded, but was not going to let her go alone. We both breathed deeply and when our lungs had absorbed all the air they could we nodded at each other, pivoted and swam for the bottom.

I opened my eyes but it was too dark to see anything and kicked toward the depths. I had no idea how deep the hole was and was almost out of air, still not having touched bottom yet. I spun my body and was about to kick for the surface when my foot hit something odd and I reached down and grabbed a frayed piece of rope. I grabbed Shayla and led her to the surface.

"What'd you do that for?" she scolded me once I had caught my breath. "I can stay longer."

"My foot hit this." I held up the piece of rope. "But it's too deep for me to see if there is anything else." Before I could stop her, she took a deep breath and was gone, leaving me treading water and waiting.

Her ability underwater amazed me and again I started to worry. I was just about to go after her when I felt movement below me and she surfaced smoothly, holding a piece of wood that looked like the top of a chest.

CHAPTER TWENTY-SEVEN

Together we walked through the shallow toward the skiff.

Rhames heard us and came over. Several of the crewmen were dragging the carcasses of two goats he had shot. "I think we've found it," I said hoarsely, the salt water I swallowed stinging my throat. I handed the piece of rope and wood to him.

"Just a piece, then?" he asked, but I could see the smile on his rugged face.

"Felt like it was part of a chest," I said. "There's more there, but it's too deep. We need to get the pump and gear."

"Aye, be good to have our assets back together again as well. Hard to trust these government types." He turned to check that the carcasses were loaded and we pushed off. The tide was slack and we coasted over the reef and rowed back to the ship.

Pierre and Mason met us at the rail and called some men over to help Rhames with the goats. I was last up the ladder. "We need to get the gear," I said and told him how we had found the cave. "It's too deep without it." I handed the piece of rotten wood to Pierre.

He took it and smiled.

The ship was underway in minutes, the mood having changed to one of cautious celebration, but that was short-lived when the rain we had been expecting started in earnest. I feared the worst when we hit the channel and the current took us, swinging the ship back and forth across the top of the whitecaps. Rain blasted the ship, streaming in horizontal waves, before finally exhausting itself. Soon the decks were steaming from the warmth of the sun and I looked up at the sky. The clouds were high and puffy, the angrier black ones moving quickly to the north.

***

The *Panther* was at anchor where we had left her, and I was surprised no work had been done to her. I started to worry, not seeing a watch, and called to her, realizing too late how far my voice carried in the quiet anchorage. There was no answer. Mason called for the sails to be furled and the anchor dropped, and Rhames readied the skiff to see what was wrong. It was just dusk, and even at anchor there should have been a watch posted. I found Blue and asked him to swim to shore to have a look while we checked the ship. Before we climbed down, I left strict orders with Red to double the watch and ready for action, but to stay dark and quiet. There were six of us in the skiff, all armed and ready to push off, when I heard Shayla from the deck.

"I'm going with you. My father was on that ship," she said and climbed down the ladder without an invitation.

The men reluctantly slid over to make room for her. We untied the painter and rowed to the *Panther*. No one greeted us and she appeared dark and empty. We secured the skiff and climbed aboard, arms ready. There was no need for caution; the deck was deserted. Rhames ordered the other men below to check the cabins and hold, but they returned a few minutes later empty-handed. Our men and the treasure were gone.

"Bloody magistrate's got his hand in this. I say we storm the bastard's house," Rhames yelled.

I shared his rage, but needed to temper his spirit. "Let Blue report back. We can get the pump and equipment in the meantime. Once he gets back we'll organize a party to go to shore." I hoped a little time might allow cooler heads to prevail. Because of the pump, we had to take two trips back to the *Caiman*, leaving Shayla and me alone on the deck waiting for the skiff to return.

"I'm worried about my father," she said accusingly. "Why are we wasting time?"

"I sent Blue to scout the village. No use to rush in until we have information. Believe me, I'm as anxious as you are."

After a brief inspection of the ship I doubted there had been any action. Everything seemed to be in order and there was no blood on the decks. "If I had to guess, I'd think the magistrate is holding them as insurance. We've been gone almost a week longer than planned."

That seemed to satisfy her, and we climbed down the ladder to the skiff that had just returned. Rhames met me on the deck of the *Caiman*. He had a cutlass swinging from his hip and two pistols jammed in his belt.

"We've got to think this through," I said, trying to gauge his mood.

"Bloody hell we do," he said. "Bastards got our treasure—and the men!"

He was deep in the embrace of the bloodlust. I had seen this before with Gasparilla's crew and knew how tricky it could be to calm them down.

"Storming the town is likely to get a lot of people killed—some of them ours." I looked at the dark water, desperate to see Blue and get his report. Rhames was about to say something when we saw a figure on the shore waving to us. From its stature I was sure it was Blue. "Let's see what he's found."

He stuck his thumbs in his gun belt and called out to the men, both assigning the shore party and setting a battle watch onboard the *Caiman*.

Swift stood by me with two other men, waiting for Rhames to finish. I saw the disappointed look on Red and Pierre's faces. "You're still hurt," I addressed Red and then turned to Pierre. "And you've got a country to save."

We armed and crept down the ladder, careful to keep our weapons from banging against the ship. Once we were aboard the skiff, I pointed to a pier near where Blue had stood by the edge of the town. There were a few lights ashore but the area where I intended to land was dark.

Just as we eased against the wood structure, Blue came out of the shadows. I thought about hiding the skiff in the brush next to the pier, but decided against it in case we needed to make a quick getaway. The tide was low, revealing the muck surrounding the shore; not something we would want to fight our way through if pursued. Following Blue in a broken line, with ten feet between us so as not to look like a gang, we entered the town. It was hard to orient myself in the darkness, and we took several wrong turns before reaching the jail. My first priority was to find Pott. If anyone knew what had happened to the crew, he would.

The guards on either side of the door quickly succumbed to Blue's blowgun and I placed Swift in one of their places, hoping he would pass as a guard to a casual observer. Blue went to check the surrounding buildings while Rhames and I moved around the back of the stone building.

"Pott," I whispered at every window, but got no reply. Thinking he must be in an interior cell, I was about to search the guards for a key when I heard a whisper.

"Is that you, Captain?"

I moved to the sound of the voice. "Aye. Can you talk?"

"The guards—"

"Handled. Tell me what you know and we'll free you."

"It's a bad business, this man. If the governor were to know what he is doing here—"

I interrupted him again, "Where are the men?"

"The crew, you mean. He's got them working the salt mine—like slaves, they are."

"And why not you?"

"Every day he comes and sits by the door, asking questions about the crown's business. The man's got ambition, that's a certainty, but how he's going about it is against the law."

I looked at Rhames. "He's safer here for the time being. We'll have to hide the guards and make it look like they wandered off on a drunk. If he's gone, it'll raise an alarm and I'd rather not have the magistrate find out we were here."

"Aye. Get out of here as fast as we can, make a plan and take the bastards. I'll be wanting a piece of his royal highness as well."

"You can't leave me here," Pott whined.

"You're safer here. Can't have you getting hurt—I've got plans for you." We walked away, leaving him uncertain of his fate, but alive. Pulling the guards behind us, we made our way back to the skiff and stashed the bodies in the mangroves.

"What of the men?" Rhames asked.

A plan had been forming in my head. "We'll have to take them by surprise. With no idea of the force here, it'd be a fool's errand otherwise."

He agreed and boarded the skiff, rowing silently to the *Caiman*. When we reached her, I ordered all the lights extinguished and the anchor raised. Under the mainsail, we slipped from the harbor. Once I was certain we were out of sight of the town, we lit a lantern and gathered around the chart.

"With the dammed reef, the only place to land men is the town," Mason said.

I studied the chart. "The north is out after our run-in with the treasure hunters there. We go here." I pointed to a cove on the south shore.

"The reef'll take us there for sure," Mason said.

"We'll have to anchor off the coast and shuttle the men across."

"That'll take all day," Rhames said.

"It might." I knew it would be a long and backbreaking task to transport twenty or so men across the reef, then navigate the large bay and land them safely. "It'll take five loads, if I've got my math correct. The first'll be the scouts. Blue and several men can go ashore and find our crew. When we're all ashore, they can lead us to them."

"Aye, we'll take the bastards at night," Rhames said.

Swift and Red nodded behind him and we began to plan the action.

***

I left Mason, Shayla, Lucy, Pierre and four of the freedmen on the ship. It had taken most of the day to shuttle the men and arms. I looked up at Shayla as the last skiff pulled away.

"Bring my father back," she called over the rail.

I turned my attention to the reef and called out direction to the men on the oars. We found a slot in the corral and were into the bay. After a half hour, we changed positions and I took my turn on the oars. It was hard work with the tide and current, but we soon landed on the beach.

"Where's Rhames?" I asked and jumped from the skiff.

"They've moved out already. He says to follow," Red said.

I was upset by his impatience and we set out over the saltpan, following the footsteps of the men that had gone before us. There was no trail and we were exposed, but the only onlookers were the hundreds of flamingos pecking at the dried salt.

We came upon the camp suddenly and dropped to the ground. The flat seemed to glow in the moonlight and I could clearly see rows of tents. Rhames came beside me. "Sentries?" I asked.

"A handful. We'll take them easily."

"No guns," I said to his dismay. "I've got a plan for after."

He grinned. "And what would that be?"

"The magistrate will get his due," I said and left it at that. "When you're ready, take the guards and I'll free the men. Get

Red and Swift to get them back to the *Caiman* and tell Mason to sail her into the harbor at noon."

"And what of us?"

"We'll take care of the magistrate." He wanted more details, but my plan was a little short in that area. "Go."

I watched from a small rise, trying to stay concealed with the little cover available. Rhames led a party to the only structure in the camp. The men quickly surrounded it and a few minutes later I saw the guards come out holding their hands high over their heads. Rhames had them secured and soon our men were moving toward us. They looked worse for the wear, their faces drawn and bodies caked with salt, and I swore the magistrate would pay for their abuse.

I waited until the column of men was well across the flat, my anger rising as several stumbled from exhaustion or abuse. We watched until they crossed over the last rise.

CHAPTER TWENTY-EIGHT

As in most Caribbean outposts, you could tell the time by the attitude of the people on the street. From the raucous behavior and the crowd in front of the pub, I expected it was late afternoon. I smiled. Having the majority of the town drunk or on their way there would make our plan simpler. We crept behind the row of buildings across the street from the pub and waited. Even from this distance we could hear the crowd, and a particularly loud voice yelled something, followed by a roar of laughter.

Using the buildings for cover, we moved to the jail. Only one man sat in front of the jail, his head bobbing in the afternoon heat, and I suspected the concealment of the bodies of the other guards had worked. Rhames crept up behind him and extended his nap with a blow to the head. He fell over and I grabbed the keys from his belt.

A blast of hot air carrying the stench of unwashed men greeted us when I opened the door. I found Pott laid out on a wooden pallet. He was barely conscious. His clothes were torn and I could see dried blood and bruises marring his face.

"Pott," I called, trying every key in the lock. With only two left, the door opened and I entered. I shook him and saw his eyes open slightly.

"Captain," he croaked.

"Can you walk?"

He swung his legs over the edge of the bunk and slowly got to his feet. "Yes."

"Let's go, then," I said, and led him into the daylight. Rhames and Blue remained in position until we were out of sight across the street.

"Would you look at that," Rhames spat when he joined us. "Bloody magistrate do that to ya?" he asked.

Pott ignored him. "They're all in the pub."

"We still have surprise with us, then," I said.

"Seems Saturday afternoons the magistrate orders a gambling contest. Every week, he'll pick someone and take their money," Pott said.

That explained the atmosphere at the pub. "Let's go," I said to Rhames and Blue. "Put the bastard out of business."

"You sure you want to meddle in the local politics?" Rhames asked. "We find where he stashed our treasure and get out of here before they sober up. The men are free and you've got the crown's lackey back."

"We need a friendly port." I tried to keep the frustration from my voice. "Pott here has the qualifications. Let's give the magistrate what he deserves and install Pott in his place."

"So, you're meddling in King Georgie's business? How do you expect that's going to end?"

"Very well, if we play this right," I answered and walked toward the pub. I dared not look behind me to see if they were following, but thought I heard the crunch of crushed coral beneath their boots.

We reached the pub and I pushed my way through the door with a swagger that I wasn't sure I could back up without Rhames behind me. The magistrate was on his knees by the far wall, a large group around him. I stood in a dark corner and watched, wanting to gauge the temper of the room before acting.

Rhames came next to me with a glass in his hand. "Throat's a bit dry," he said. "Blue's watching over the weasel outside."

I felt better with him at my side. A loud cheer came up from the crowd and I saw the magistrate rise to his feet and accept a wad of money from his victim. I slid further into the shadows and bumped someone.

"Best watch where you're stepping," he said. The man had a defeated look about him.

"Sorry. Can we buy you a drink?" He nodded and I asked Rhames to get a glass.

"Bastard's taken my pay again," he said.

"You mean the magistrate?" I asked.

"He lines us up every Saturday after pay call and choses a few men to play. There's no escaping his wrath if you don't abide him. And if you're lucky enough not to get chosen you'd better cheer for him or you're likely to be next."

"How does he win all the time?" I asked and caught a look from Rhames that showed my naivety. He handed the man a glass and we waited while he drained it.

"You there!" someone yelled.

I looked around the room and saw the crowd part, leaving a clear path between the magistrate and me. There was nowhere to hide.

"You're the captain of those ships." He waddled toward me, obviously drunk.

I knew from experience how dangerous drunks could be and played him carefully. "We came looking for you to honor our agreement," I said, trying to defuse the situation.

"Our agreement, you say." He grabbed a glass from a man nearby and drank the amber liquid in one swallow. "Our agreement was for you to make me rich!"

Laughter came from the crowd, but it sounded forced. "We've had little luck," I said.

"That may be the case, but you've a load of treasure in your holds."

The crowd was getting nervous now and moved backwards, leaving us alone in the center of the room. I couldn't blame Pott for talking after seeing the torture inflicted on him, but I had a problem now.

He moved toward me and I could smell the rum on his breath. "And I've claimed it for the crown."

I had to make a stand or I would find myself with a rope around my neck. "For the crown or for yourself?"

The crowd murmured and he looked around for support. His hand went to his belt, but Rhames was by his side. "Maybe the two of you should settle this like men," he said.

"Who …" the magistrate started, but was drowned out by the roar of the crowd.

I was getting uneasy about this, not being a gambler myself and knowing Rhames's tendency toward losing. "What are you doing?" I whispered to him.

"Don't worry, I've got your back," he said and cleared a path to the wall.

The group gathered tightly around us and I started to panic.

"We'll let the captain play first, then," Rhames said. The crowd cheered and he grabbed the dice from the magistrate's hand.

The crowd cheered and Rhames handed me the dice. "Just throw them—they're fixed."

"But …" I was suffocated by the crowd, moving closer now, anxious to see the magistrate's dice that had taken their money played against him. I rolled the two cubes in my hand and readied to throw when I felt the knife against my ribs.

"Not so fast."

The magistrate's blade pierced my shirt. Rhames and the other men were too busy waiting for me to roll the dice to see what was happening.

"Me and the young captain here are going outside to have a private conversation," he said, pushing me in front of him toward the door. I had no illusions about what this talk would consist of and looked behind me, hoping Rhames could intervene, but he was lost in the crowd.

I knew I was on my own. Although not a fighter by nature, I had drilled in hand-to-hand combat with the rest of Gasparilla's crew. Counting on the magistrate's drunkenness to play to my advantage, I stopped at the threshold and looked back. In the instant the magistrate followed my gaze, I jammed my elbow into his stomach and spun around. I went for his knife arm and grabbed the elbow in an attempt to twist it behind his head, but before I could execute the move, he roared and grabbed me in a bear hug. I could feel the tip of the knife start to dig into my stomach.

Just as the blade pieced my skin I lifted my foot and slammed the heel of my boot into his knee. He fell backward and I turned on him, but Rhames had made his way through the crowd and stood over the fallen man, his boot on his chest. I stood back, trying to catch my breath, and heard the crowd, their bloodlust high, seeing their enemy in dire straits. They were pressing closer and I could tell they were about to take the situation into their own hands.

A shot fired. Everyone stopped and looked around, their eyes finally focusing on Blue, who stood in the doorway grinning with a pistol in each hand.

The crowd moved backward as Blue entered the room. Rhames went to him and took the pistols, waving one at the crowd and the other on the magistrate. "You'll listen to the captain, then."

The room was quiet now and I moved to a clear space and stood on a chair. "Killing this man will bring you no relief. The governor will find out and, before he knows the facts, will send troops." I had their attention now. "I have a man that is educated in these matters, that can take charge." I pointed to the magistrate. "Let the crown's justice take care of him. How many of you has he stolen from or abused?" Men nodded and several spoke out. "How many?" I repeated, louder this time. More men chimed in and soon there was a chorus in the room.

I waited for them to quiet. "Let all of you testify and he will get the justice he deserves." A roar came from the crowd and several men came forward, taking the magistrate between them. They dragged him to his feet and pulled him out of the pub. The crowd moved outside, following behind the men as they paraded him to the jail.

CHAPTER TWENTY-NINE

I could tell Pott was uneasy standing next to me in front of the jail. The magistrate was incarcerated and I meant to assign his replacement before the mood of the crowd changed. Aside from being my man, he was certainly qualified for the position after his years of service under the governor of the Caymans. He knew the political machinations of the British government and was familiar with the governor of the Bahamas. Along with the testimony of the town, he would add his own, surely incriminating the magistrate.

The crowd went their own ways, with only a few hangers-on, wanting to be the first to lobby Pott for favor. They followed behind us as we walked to the magistrate's house.

"This is it, then," I said to him as we stood outside the door.

"I can't thank you enough for what you've done for me," he said.

"Don't worry about that, there will come a time, Magistrate Pott." We said our goodbyes. I promised to return in a few days and let him know the status of our search. Although the crew might not like it, I meant to honor my agreement with the previous magistrate and pay over part of the treasure to the government. At least I knew with Pott, it would go where it was intended and solidify his position.

It was dark when we reached the *Caiman*, now anchored in the harbor. Shayla was sitting with Phillip by the rail, watching the residents celebrate the fall of the magistrate. I stayed with them for a while.

"I'm off to bed," I said, expecting her to join me.

"I think I'll spend some time with my father," she said.

I could hear the celebration from my bunk. Tossing and turning, I found no rest until Shayla joined me.

***

The morning was much like yesterday and I feared we would have to face several squalls. We left Mason with the *Panther* to resume the work on her. Rhames had been up early and had enlisted the help of several fishing boats to return our treasure to her hold. Later than I would have liked, we set off in the *Caiman* for the cove on the small island. I spent most of the trip going through the dive gear, cleaning and oiling the fittings and hoses.

We arrived without incident and anchored outside the cove. I checked the skies and saw no threat of weather, but I pressed the crew to ready the skiff and gear. The sooner we recovered whatever was here and were on our way, the better. I paced the deck impatiently, waiting for the tide to turn, allowing us to cross the reef and enter the cove.

Shayla accompanied us. Her previous underwater exploits had spread through the crew and I thought if we did recover the treasure this might be the way to get her the share she deserved.

With Swift, Blue and two other crewmen on the oars, it was a tight fit with the gear, and I worried about making it over the reef with this much weight. Fortunately it was almost the same time as yesterday, and with the high tide we able to skirt the coral.

I surveyed the cave from the skiff and decided it would be better to set up the pump on land. Two crewmen who had helped me recover the ballast from the wreck in the Caymans were assigned to set up and monitor the equipment. After a few minutes of fiddling with the valves, they gave me the thumbs-up. I donned the leather helmet and adjusted the glass plate. I felt the now-familiar whoosh of fresh air enter the headgear and returned the signal, then entered the water.

The weights attached to my waist brought me to the bottom faster than I expected and I had to take a few minutes to allow the pressure in my ears to subside. As I stood on the sandy bottom adjusting to the depth, I watched small fish peck at the sharp coral walls that extended down from the exposed rocks above.

I walked on the sandy bottom toward the cave's entrance and, once inside, waited for my eyes to acclimate to the darkness. Barley able to see the walls around me, I slid my feet forward in the direction of the hole. The bottom dropped off and I went to my knees before sliding my body backwards into the recess, stopping when my feet landed on wood. The hole was narrow here and I had to fight with the gear and hoses to turn myself facedown. On my belly, I slid down to the chests. I could feel the wood, but it was too dark to see anything.

Something swam by my head and, when I tried to see what it was, my headgear jammed in a recess in the wall. I struggled with the awkward equipment, fighting for breath. Finally, by twisting my head and upper body, I was able to free myself, but not before tearing the air hose from the headgear. Bubbles surrounded me as the men above continued to pump, not knowing my distress. I reached for the end of the flailing hose, grabbed it and fought blindly to find the grommet where it had come from. Finally, almost out of breath, I found the hole and inserted the hose. I sat on the bottom, trying to even out my breath and slow my racing mind. The tight space and darkness were more difficult than I anticipated.

Calmer now, I turned my body and went headfirst to the bottom. Darkness surrounded me and I had to work by feel. My hand touched wood. Rotten from the seawater, it pulled away easily, the nails and straps having rusted away. I removed the plank, set it to the side and reached my hand into the opening. My hopes surged when I felt the smooth metal and struggled to pull a bar free. With the first of what I hoped were many, I worked backwards out of the cave and surfaced with the bar clutched tightly in my hand.

Unable to talk until the headgear was removed, I handed the bar to Shayla and heard her gasp. Mason and Blue worked the leather enclosure off my head and I was soon staring at the gold bar.

"How many?" Mason asked.

"Three, maybe four chests," I answered and watched them as they passed the bar around. "Right then. We need a system to get it out of there. It's in a hellish space, I'll need help."

Mason sent the skiff back to the ship with orders to bring rope and netting. While we waited, I lay with my shirt off in the sun, trying to warm up. The water had been colder than I expected. Shayla lay next to me and I guessed we were both dreaming about the pile of gold we were about to bring to light. The skiff returned and I gave orders to the new men. Suited up again, I was soon back in the water, clasping a light line in my hand. I was to secure it as best I could to allow Shayla an easy path to retrieve the treasure. With my other hand, I pulled a bundle of netting and line behind me.

I entered the cave again, on my belly this time, and slithered across the sandy bottom. It took a little longer moving in this fashion, but it eliminated the need to turn around. Before descending the last few feet to the gold, I spread out the net on the closest flat spot, hoping I would be able to reach it from below, and slid to the bottom. I pried the remaining boards and set them out of the way, then reached in and started to remove the gold bars. By reaching behind me, I was able to set them in the net, allowing Shayla to take the line to the surface, where the men hauled the chests up. I quickly lost count of the bars and worked mindlessly until my hands were raw and all the gold was removed before ascending. The first thing I saw after the headgear was off was the huge pile of golden bars on the rocks.

It took three loads to get the treasure, men and equipment back to the ship. When the gold came aboard I heard the cheers of the crew, but our celebration was cut short when the watch spotted storm clouds on the horizon. I wanted to reach the safety of the town's harbor before they hit. We were underway in minutes and, with the wind on a beam reach, were soon away from the small island. I collapsed onto the deck and leaned against the rail, exhausted.

***

* * *

An hour later I heard the calls to furl the sails and the anchor splashed. I rose from the deck, my mouth dry, but feeling refreshed. My thirst sated from several ladles of water, I went to the helm. Mason and Rhames were talking, but stopped when I approached.

"Something wrong?" I asked.

"Back to Haiti?" Rhames asked.

"Thought you'd lost your taste for the island," I answered.

"We have some unfinished business there if you're going," Rhames said.

CHAPTER THIRTY

I almost didn't recognize my own ship when we entered the harbor. Mason had the *Panther* just about finished and the change was impressive. He had found some paint in town, and with new colors on the trim and gunports I doubted she would be recognized.

I split the pirates between the ships. We had decided that it was better to take both ships. The governor of the Caymans, from what I knew of him, was not about to let us vanish. Whether he had found out we sunk his frigate or not, he knew of the treasure in our holds and would likely have alerted his counterpart in Jamaica by now. Soon the word would spread and the *Panther* would be taken on sight. With both ships we would be able to defend ourselves.

There were several things that required attention, but they could wait. I wanted this adventure over and did not want the *Panther* out of my sight again. After a day and a half of clean sailing, we reached the coast of Haiti. It was my first inclination to send scouts ashore until I knew it was safe for Pierre. I had fought for his safety, but in the end he won and led the shore party. He was desperate to set foot on his home soil and see

Cloe. Blue and I would stay with the skiff in case he needed to make a fast escape.

"Swift and I's going with him," Rhames said.

I thought I knew what they were after now. "Right then. But don't interfere."

Both ships anchored off the coast near the river we had made our escape from, and along with two French-speaking crewmen, we rowed ashore. Once past the surf at the inlet, we pulled to the west shore and watched Pierre, Rhames and Swift disappear into the brush, leaving Blue and me to the mosquitos.

***

I could hear giggling coming from the trail, and seconds later Rhames appeared, ushering three of the women ahead of him. Swift and a strange man followed. "I see you got what you came for," I said to Rhames. "But three?"

In truth, I hoped the women would settle the men down some.

"Can't leave Red out of the party, now can we?"

The stranger came forward and introduced himself. "Mr. Pierre is secure in the palace. He will be here at first light with carts and men."

The man went on tell us that Cloe had held the palace, rallying the guards to Pierre's cause in his absence, but the president in the South now held the Citadel. This was troubling news, but at least Pierre still held a foothold of power, though I suspected, after seeing the Citadel, that he would need more than the share of gold to take it.

* * *

Haitian Gold

***

I couldn't believe the transformation when I saw Pierre standing on the beach the next morning. In uniform, with Cloe by his side, he looked the part of a leader. Shayla and I rowed out to meet them and sent the skiff back to the *Caiman* to bring his share of the gold. Cloe stood by him and interpreted for us.

"The president in the South wants to reunite the country as one. He has taken the Citadel and with the fortress in his possesion, we will not be able to take him," Pierre said.

It was an odd reunion with his station changed and both of us knew this might be the last time we saw each other. "Surely your share of the gold would be enough to buy men and arms?" I asked.

"Maybe it would, but the fight would leave the country destitute. It is better for Haiti to have a united country than one devastated by civil war. The French would surely use that opportunity to attack."

"Do you have a plan, then?"

"The president is rumored to be a good man. It is my thought to speak with him and unite the country," he said proudly.

"But you would lose power."

"The gold will buy me power and influence, if not with a high position in government then as the richest man in Haiti," he laughed. "And it is better to be a rich free man than a poor French slave."

I had to agree with him. He was last to leave and we stood on the trail together, watching the heavily guarded mule cart struggle to make its way up the hill to the castle, and embraced.

"You are always welcome here," he said.

"And when they throw you out, there will be a spot on the crew for you," I replied and we laughed.

"Where are you off to?"

"Back to Inagua. I've got some politics to handle."

"Good luck to you," he said.

"And you, my friend."

***

We were halfway across the channel. Haiti's mountains were still visible behind us, and the low form of Great Inagua had just appeared ahead. It was a quiet ship, with everyone exhausted from the last week, when the watch spotted a sail.

I climbed into the rigging with the glass and froze when I saw the Union Jack and the distinctive shape of the governor's schooner.

"Get all the canvas we have up and call to the *Caiman* to do the same," I yelled to the deck.

At once the ship picked up speed. We were on a collision course, the schooner looking to have just come from Inagua. "Load the guns. It's going to be close." There was a flurry of activity on deck. I looked over to the *Caiman* and saw the same. With two ships this would be an easier fight.

I waited, watching the schooner as the ships converged, and stared in surprise when the schooner veered away.

"She doesn't know us," Mason yelled up.

The work on the *Panther* had paid off and for the first time in months, I felt like a free man.

Made in the USA
Middletown, DE
14 August 2016